"I never…"

Tenley trailed off and lifted her head to the sky. She rode with her eyes closed, trusting her horse in a way that was pure Tenley. It ripped away the last of the bandages covering Mac's scabbed heart and exposed him to the light.

Mac's pulse skipped. "What?" The need to hear her answer shouldn't hook straight into his heart. But it did. "You never what?" He ground out the question, desperate for an answer.

She met his gaze head-on. "I never stopped." She shook her head, a sad look entering her eyes. "What I did, I did for your own good."

"Funny how I can't believe that." He reined his horse sideways, putting space between them. Her response fueled more questions. "I never wanted to come back here." He rolled the stiffness from his shoulder.

"So why did you?"

"Jade." His niece's name rolled from him like thunder through the sky. "She's all I have now, and I'll protect her with everything I have."

"Even from me."

Tabitha Bouldin has a bachelor's degree in creative writing/English from Southern New Hampshire University. She is a member of American Christian Fiction Writers (ACFW) and an avid reader when her three cats will allow her to pick up a book. Living in Tennessee her entire life, Tabitha grew up riding horses and adopting every stray animal she could find.

Books by Tabitha Bouldin

Love Inspired

The Cowgirl's Last Rodeo
Forgiving the Cowboy

FORGIVING THE COWBOY

TABITHA BOULDIN

Love Inspired
INSPIRATIONAL ROMANCE

 **LOVE INSPIRED**®
INSPIRATIONAL ROMANCE

ISBN-13: 978-1-335-93704-9

Recycling programs
for this product may
not exist in your area.

Forgiving the Cowboy

Copyright © 2025 by Tabitha Bouldin

Love Inspired
22 Adelaide St. West, 41st Floor
Toronto, Ontario M5H 4E3, Canada
www.LoveInspired.com

Printed in Lithuania

MIX
Paper | Supporting
responsible forestry
FSC® C021394

Trust in the Lord with all thine heart; and lean not unto thine own understanding. In all thy ways acknowledge him, and he shall direct thy paths.
—*Proverbs* 3:5–6

For my sister. It takes a strong woman to stand up every day and fight for her happily-ever-after. You are that woman, and your daily fight is an inspiration that encourages me to keep going, especially when life is hard.

Chapter One

Tenley Jacobs had a major problem on her hands. She sighed and threaded the chewed-up scraps of leather through her palms. "You're in big trouble." She waved what used to be bridle reins at the rambunctious puppy bounding up and down the barn aisle. Unconcerned, the white German shepherd pounced on a patch of hay and yipped, tail wagging, little bottom wriggling left and right in a wild arc, as he looked back at Tenley. "Don't give me that look. I'm mad at you."

"Aw. Aunt Tenley, he didn't mean it." Six-year-old Jade Matthews added a whine to the new "aunt" title and dropped into a crouch beside the puppy. Her bright green eyes lit up with the first bit of joy Tenley had seen in weeks.

"Sure, he didn't." She tossed the mangled reins onto a hay bale and rubbed her hands over her face. They smelled of oil and leather. The familiar scent soaked into her bones, attempting to right the whirlwind the day had become.

Freckles, a leopard-spotted Appaloosa and Jade's equine therapy partner, whinnied from the stall at the far end of the barn, drawing Tenley's gaze toward the sunlight streaming in through the open double doors. "Come on.

We need to start your lesson." She held out a hand in a stop motion. "But first, put your dog in the empty stall."

Jade opened her mouth, an argument brewing, with a look so much like her mother that it staggered Tenley and forced her to hug her elbows over her stomach to keep from throwing her arms around Jade and squeezing tight. Jade had been withdrawn since her parents' deaths, and Tenley didn't dare risk ostracizing her by offering unwanted comfort. Jade had made her feelings clear the first time Tenley gave an unexpected embrace.

Tenley hiked an eyebrow and put a hand on her hip. "That was the deal. You get the dog, but he stays out of the way. Especially when we're acclimating new horses. Or when someone is riding. Like you're supposed to be doing." Freckles nickered again, his trumpeting sound echoing through the barn. The Appaloosa gelding was Tenley's newest acquisition for her equine therapy program, and he'd quickly become Jade's favorite horse to ride. His only problem seemed to be an aversion to being alone—hence the constant nickering. A problem Tenley remedied by placing him in a stall beside Socks, a large black-and-white gelding who was as unflustered as they came. Currently, Socks didn't seem too thrilled with his new neighbor and was busy ignoring Freckles' need for attention.

"Will you let me ride Freckles on a trail ride?" Jade scooped the puppy into her arms and huffed when he wriggled. At eight months old, the pup was half Jade's length, and when he started flailing all four paws, he became almost impossible to hold. Jade shuffled toward the open stall door and dropped the puppy to the thick bed of straw. Before she could jump back and close the door, the pup shot between her feet and darted into the hallway. He lowered his front half and stuck his tail up in the air. It waved side to side, and he barked at Jade, his head bouncing when he jumped and took off running outside.

And that's why Tenley had resisted getting the dog in the first place. She worked with therapy horses. Her brother, Brody, was the horse trainer, but neither of them knew anything about training dogs. Her family's sole experience with canines came from owning a few random work dogs through the years to help keep coyotes away.

Tenley plodded after the runaway canine and stepped into the bright sunshine that coated the Triple Bar Ranch in a golden glow. The Blue Ridge Mountains poked their heads up in the distance, drawing Tenley's gaze. She loved her North Carolina home with a depth that filled her to bursting. Wild horses couldn't drag her away from the ranch she'd always called home. Especially not now that she'd finally gotten her equine therapy license and opened her own clinic alongside Brody's horse training barn.

Laughter drifted on the breeze from the round pen, and Tenley caught a flash of movement between the tall panels. Her brother Brody and his wife, Callie, worked a new horse together, their joy permeating the air and drawing a smile to Tenley's face.

Jade raced after the wayward dog, her steps light and quick. "Get back here you rascal."

"Maybe that's what we should call him." Tenley swiped a hand over her forehead, drawing away a line of sweat before it trickled into her eyes. Less than two weeks into May and the summer heat had already turned vicious. Winter could not come soon enough. She loved living in the shadow of the Blue Ridge Mountains, but she was tired of the heat and humidity that came with it. Give her snow any day.

Jade caught up with the pup and dove on top of him. They rolled in the dirt, laughter and doggie yips colliding.

Tenley grabbed the discarded bridle reins and hurried over, using them as a makeshift leash that she quickly tied to the pup's collar. "Take him to the stall, Jade."

Jade's lower lip stuck out in a pout, but she followed Tenley's directions.

Tenley tagged along behind her, doing her best to stay out of the way and let the girl find a measure of independence. Even at almost seven years old, Jade had her mother's stubborn streak.

Jade led the pup to the stall, removed the temporary leash and closed the door before he could escape. She handed the leather strip to Tenley and hurried down the aisle to Freckles' stall with a big smile on her face. "Don't worry. We can ride now." She flung open the door and reached for the halter.

The gentle gelding followed Jade to the crossties and stood statue still while Jade brushed him down. She dragged the tall stool they kept for the younger, shorter riders over and began saddling and bridling him. Freckles settled under Jade's attention.

Emotion clogged Tenley's throat at the sight of Freckles leaning his head down to bump Jade's shoulder. She patted his jaw, then flung her arms around his neck and squeezed. Now, a horse, she would hug. This was why Tenley pushed for the equine therapy program. Not just for Jade, but for all the hurting people who could benefit from the horses.

She'd been one of those hurting people. A closet alcoholic who'd hit rock bottom and found herself sitting overnight in a jail cell in Bridgeport instead of getting ready to walk down the aisle. Thankfully, she hadn't hurt anyone, but the drunk-and-disorderly had kept her behind bars for her wedding day, and once she was released, she'd been too ashamed to tell Mac Mitchell, her fiancé, the truth about why she'd jilted him at the altar. She wasn't even coherent enough to make a phone call from jail... The memory stung intensely.

In the immediate aftermath, he up and left for Chicago without a goodbye or a backward glance.

He was clearly too hurt and too proud to fight for her. She couldn't really blame him though, not when her pride kept her in a prison of her own making. And she hadn't been ready to fight for him either. Not until it was too late.

Over six years of silence followed, and every year that passed made it that much harder to make amends. Even though she had six years, eleven months, and seven days sober under her belt and God's forgiveness in her heart, she doubted Mac would be able to see his way clear of her indiscretion. She didn't deserve his forgiveness. Or her dad's. She was the reason he'd been out driving the day of the hit-and-run and had been paralyzed. It was all her fault.

Her pulse hammered in her throat as she watched Jade. Amber, Jade's mother, was Mac's sister and Tenley's best friend. She'd named Tenley and Mac as Jade's guardians in her will when she found out she was pregnant. She'd given birth shortly before Tenley and Mac's wedding. Once things fell apart, Tenley had assumed that Amber changed the will.

According to Leonard, the lawyer who'd sought Tenley out after Amber's fatal car accident, she hadn't. Tenley and Mac shared guardianship of Amber's daughter— married or not.

Mac hadn't shown up for the funeral, a fact that needled Tenley to no end. She couldn't wait to hear his excuse when he finally did arrive. And she knew he would. Eventually. Her past forever lingered in the background of her thoughts. Mac's imminent return kept things churned up. The apology she'd never given, the reason she'd never explained. He deserved to know the truth, even if he never forgave her for running away. For once in her life, she'd protected him instead of letting him fight her battles for her. This was one battle she'd had to face herself. No one else could achieve sobriety for her.

She bit her lip until she tasted blood. Did he know they shared guardianship? Did he care? Leonard had tried to call Mac, but the last he'd mentioned to Tenley, Mac was unavailable for some reason he wouldn't disclose. When she pressed for further information, Leonard had given her a look that bordered on pity and said he'd keep in touch.

Jade finished tacking up her horse, snapped her helmet on, and peered over her shoulder, a smile blooming and showing the gap where she'd lost her front tooth last week.

"I'm ready." Jade patted Freckles' leg and waited.

Tenley nodded. "Okay. Take him out to the small arena. You can mount up at the gate, and I'll close it behind you."

Tenley allowed Jade to have slightly more control over the lesson than a lot of her other students, except when Jade joined them in a group ride. Unlike the others, Jade had grown up riding at the ranch, with Tenley as her teacher. These lessons on Freckles were more for Jade's psychological well-being than anything else.

Which brought Tenley back to Jade's earlier question about riding Freckles on a trail ride. Tenley hesitated to say no. Freckles was trained to take anything in stride, but trail rides were different. Anything could happen out on the trail.

Jade led Freckles from the barn, paused at the mounting block and climbed into the saddle. Once on Freckles' back, she shot another winning smile at Tenley and moved into the arena.

They spent the next twenty minutes going through Tenley's preplanned lesson. Jade walked, trotted and loped Freckles around the arena, her concentration showing in the way she frowned and sucked her bottom lip between her teeth. Just like her mother.

Tenley walked alongside her as she led Freckles from the arena and back to the crossties, where they removed the gelding's tack, rubbed him down and put him back in his stall.

"Alright, let's head to the house." Tenley opened the stall door where the puppy waited, tail furiously sweeping the ground.

Jade whooped and raced outside.

Tenley kept her pace slower, enjoying the slight breeze rustling the oak leaves on the trees lining the trails to her left. Her parents' house sat at the end of the long drive. Tenley's house was situated the farthest away from the main house and the barn. Her brother and Callie lived in the house behind the barn, and her sister Molly had chosen to build hers on the southern side of the yard, directly across from it. Molly lived there with her young son, Luke, who had turned out to be a great playmate for Jade. It had been hard on them losing Luke's dad overseas, but things were getting better. Grief was a long road.

"Uncle Mac!" Jade screamed and bolted for the main house.

"Jade, wait." Mac was here? Tenley's heart pounded in

her chest, and fear shot through her like a runaway horse. Tenley ran after her, her boots slamming the packed dirt and sending jarring jolts up her legs. She shielded her eyes from the sunlight bouncing off her parents' tin roof and saw a tall man standing on their front porch.

A rangy canine stood at his side, ears up and alert, posture stiff.

"Jade," Tenley called again when the little girl continued her race down the rutted drive. Tenley stepped in a hole and stumbled several steps before she regained her balance.

The man on the porch never moved. He might as well be carved from stone.

Not Tenley. Everything in her seemed to go to war. Her heart raced, but she blamed that on the unexpected exercise. He'd finally come. She'd known he would but had hoped and prayed that she'd be given some kind of warning first. She didn't want to see him like this, out of the blue, totally unprepared. Her hands curled into fists.

Jade skidded to a stop at the bottom of the steps. "You brought Zeus." She flung her arms around the dog's neck and squeezed.

Zeus let out a pained whine.

Mac shifted his weight, and Tenley caught the flash of a grimace in his brown eyes. "Careful. He's not feeling well." He studiously ignored Tenley and kept his attention on Jade. Some unnamable emotion caught in his expression.

"What's wrong with him?" Jade ran her hands over Zeus's black-and-tan fur. Her brows wrinkled together in a perfect imitation of Mac. "Was he hurt?"

Tenley managed to stop before she hurtled into the porch railing. Gravel spewed under her boots, and her hat slid down over her forehead. She adjusted the black Stetson with one hand and shoved the other into her pocket while attempting to calm her breathing. She'd neglected her running lately, and it showed.

"Yes." Mac left it at that and finally, *finally* lifted his gaze to Tenley. His shoulders snapped back, and his lips tightened into a flat line. "Tenley."

She dipped her head into a nod. "Good to see you, Mac."

"Is it?" He asked sarcastically. His black hair looked the same with its close-cut sides that resembled a high and tight but longer. He wore jeans and a rumpled T-shirt that bore a Chicago PD logo. The sight snagged her breath and forced her chin up.

She didn't have the heart to argue with him. Not about this, though questions flickered in his expression before his eyes shuttered.

Maybe someday he'd ask. And maybe someday she'd tell him why she left him at the altar. But not today.

The puppy bounded up the steps and plopped onto its back, paws up in the air. It batted at Zeus's nose and tried to nibble the older dog's leg.

Zeus let out an almost human sigh, then lifted his head toward Mac as though asking permission. Mac made a hand movement, and Zeus lowered to his belly on the worn-out porch. Seconds ticked past, the roar in Tenley's ears filling her head as questions bombarded her from the inside.

Mom stepped out onto the porch. "Oh, Tenley, there you are. I was about to call the barn."

Dad rolled out behind Mom, his wheelchair bumping over the wooden planks. "Well, Mac, how are things in Chicago?"

"Hectic." Mac seemed determined to keep his responses short and clipped.

Tenley locked her jaw to keep from saying anything she'd regret. Mom and Dad didn't need her interference. She sat on the bottom step and drew her knees up to her chest, then stretched them out, loosening the tight muscles before they cramped. She really should start running again. Especially if she wanted to have a prayer of keeping up with Jade. Speaking of prayer, Tenley sent up a rapid-fire entreaty for guidance and peace.

"Leonard told me Jade was here with Tenley." Again, Mac's tone said more than the words themselves. He drew himself up to his full height, an impressive six foot two to her five foot seven.

Tenley resisted the urge to curl her shoulders up around her ears. The need to defend herself roared up and threatened to choke her. Not now. Not like this.

"Jade, why don't you come inside and have a glass of milk. I made cookies. They should be cool by now." Mom shepherded Jade into the house while giving Tenley a look that Tenley interpreted to mean she'd better get on the ball with smoothing the raging river of turmoil between her and Mac.

Easier said than done, but she'd try.

Relief skirted the edges of her anger, and she mouthed *thank you* over Jade's head. They disappeared inside, with Dad lingering the longest, his gaze darting back and forth between Tenley and Mac. Then he left them to it. The screen door smacked closed with the squeal of hinges in desperate need of oil.

She shifted sideways and put her booted feet on the step. "Jade is always here with me, except when she's at school." She filled her voice with accusation, the tone hot enough to blister. "It's what Amber wanted." So much for staying calm.

A dry laugh left Mac. "No. What my sister wanted was for me to take care of Jade." He waved a sheaf of papers in her direction.

Tenley snatched them from his hand and scanned the documents. Did he have a different will from the one Leonard showed her? Her breath locked in her throat. This could not be happening. Her mouth dropped open, and she snapped it closed just as quickly as relief overwhelmed her. It was the same will. "Take another look. I think you missed something." She handed them back. "Both our names are there."

Mac forced his gaze away from Tenley and back to the document. The papers crinkled in his hands as his grip tightened.

Tenley cleared her throat and rocked her boots back and forth. Heel to toe. Heel to toe. She wrapped her arms around her knees and pulled them under her chin. A breath whooshed out when she lowered her cheek to her knee and stared out over the yard. She wore a pair of tattered jeans with a rip in the knee and a T-shirt with their old school mascot on the back. Same old Tenley. She never threw away anything that might be useful later.

When they planned their wedding, she'd refurbished the majority of the decorations from yard sales and thrift stores, remaking them into beautiful pieces. Given what she'd done with ratty flowers and old ribbon, he'd been curious to see what her wedding dress would look like. He'd never found out.

He bit down on the wrenching feeling tearing open the wound she'd made the day she left him standing at the altar. Alone. No reason. No apology. She'd disappeared from the church and his life without a word. He couldn't let her distract him from his mission. From Jade. The last person he had in the world who mattered to him.

Straightening his shoulders despite the pain stiffening his arm, he brought the papers up to eye level. Tenley's name leaped from the page. Right beside his. The internal wound ripped apart, leaving him breathless. How many years had he dreamed of seeing her name beside his? Only in his dreams, it was a marriage certificate that held the honor of placing them side by side.

Not this. He shook his head. "Amber never changed the will." He should've known. Leonard tried to give him a warning. Mac had brushed off the older man's attempt with a stiff wave and bolted from the tiny office that stifled him.

It had taken all his inner strength—and the fact he was a police officer—to keep him from breaking the speed limit when Leonard told him where to find Jade.

This could not stand.

Tenley didn't deserve the right to raise Jade. She was irresponsible. She wasn't mature enough. A slew of other belittlements bombarded Mac. He locked them behind his teeth and massaged the pain shooting down his arm.

Zeus looked up at Mac and whined. The puppy continued to gnaw at Zeus's ear, but the older dog didn't seem to mind. Mac reached down to ruffle the dog's ears, reassuring his partner that he was fine.

Zeus lowered his head again, then wagged his bushy tail.

Shock coursed through Mac. It was the first time Zeus had shown any emotion other than concern since they'd both gotten injured. It made him want to call his boss and report the good news. Zeus didn't need to be retired. He wasn't too old for the job. He hadn't burned out. Neither had Mac.

Sitting with her legs drawn up, Tenley rubbed her cheek back and forth over her knee several times before lifting her head "We're both her guardians. It's right there in black-and-white."

What? Oh, right. The papers. Jade. Guardianship. He'd almost forgotten in the sudden flurry of emotion that erupted in him over bringing Zeus back to work on the force.

"No." Mac sliced a hand through the air. A hiss of pain accompanied the movement, and Tenley's eyes narrowed.

She rolled to her feet and stared up at him from the bottom of the steps. "What's wrong?"

Their different heights, along with the fact he stood on the top step and she on the bottom, put her at a disadvantage. Or it would have if she were anyone other than Tenley. She gave him a look, scouring him from head to toe before her dark brown eyes found his.

"My sister allowed you to be part of her will. That's what's wrong." He refused to let her see his pain. Pain she'd caused and pain from the bullet wound that had left a hole in his shoulder and put him off the police force for the next few months. Or so the official statement from his boss read. The unofficial one bit deeper. Those things were no longer her business. He rolled the stiffness from his neck. "I'm taking Jade back to Chicago with me."

"Nope." Tenley stomped up the steps and slammed her hands onto her hips. Her eyes met his and fire sparked in the depths. "You can't take her from everything she knows and drop her into a place like Chicago. I won't allow it.

She has two weeks of school left. You can't consider yanking her out now and forcing her to start in a new school."

"You won't—" Disbelief forced out a raw laugh. He shook the papers. "This means nothing. You have no right to be her guardian. I'm her uncle. You're *not* family." Tenley's face turned redder than a Rhode Island Red. "And I'll take care of her from now on."

"You can't go against Amber's wishes. We're both on that paper. That gives me as much right to keep her here— blood family or not." Stubbornness glinted in her eyes, and her jaw jutted forward. When she tipped her chin up and gave him that glare from their high school days, he forced himself to look away before he could give in to the emotions ricocheting around his insides.

He stepped closer, forcing her to bend her head back to meet his gaze. "My sister," his voice grumbled, "thought we would be married when she signed this." He shouldn't be so petty, but it felt good. "We'll see what a judge thinks." He refolded the papers and tucked them into his back pocket. "I'm going to see my niece now." Without another word, he yanked open the screen door and stepped inside.

Voices drifted in from the kitchen, Jade's childish laughter cutting through his belligerence and hammering home the truth. His sister was gone.

Grief sliced him. He heaved it aside and forced his lips into a smile while crossing the living room.

The door slammed behind him, and Tenley's presence filled the room. It had always been that way for him. He'd loved her. Man, how he'd loved her. And losing her had nearly destroyed him. If not for the job in Chicago and his work with K-9s in the police force during those early years…he didn't want to think about where he might've ended up.

Then he'd found Laura, and the future brightened. They'd had three years of marriage together before she passed, and the years of grief in between didn't prepare him for losing his sister.

Nothing—absolutely nothing—prepared him for seeing his high school sweetheart for the first time in almost seven years.

He waited for her to speak, but she seemed content to loiter behind him. No doubt she had her arms crossed and wore a frown that didn't fit her always congenial expression.

Shaking away the thoughts, Mac eased toward the kitchen. He paused at the entryway and leaned his good shoulder on the doorframe.

Jade sat at the kitchen table, a plate of cookies inches from her hand.

Peter and Margaret sat on either side, half-drunk glasses of milk lining the center of the table.

Peter winked at Margaret. "I don't know, dear. I think she's won." He tapped his fingers on the arm of his wheelchair. His gaze skimmed Mac, then settled on Tenley. Tight lines fanned from his mouth as he frowned, but he quickly schooled his expression and returned his attention to Jade.

"You think so?" Margaret tilted her head from side to side and dropped her hand to Jade's arm. "The goal was to see who could blow the most bubbles in their milk." She hiked one eyebrow into an arch. "I count five in mine."

"I had seven." Jade scooted to the edge of her chair and grabbed her glass of milk. She eyed it, the look of disdain so like Amber that it clenched Mac's heart into a vice grip. "One popped when I set it down. But it still counts, right?"

"What do you think, Mac?" Peter rolled away from the table and waved a hand for Mac to join them. "Do popped bubbles count?"

"They never did when I played." Pain skirted around his shoulder and sent twinges into his fingers. He tucked his hand into his pocket before they could see him flex the pain away.

Jade's glass hit the table with a clatter, and she stared at him, mouth hanging open. "You played?"

"Sure I did." He gave her a lazy grin. "No one could ever beat me. That's why they had to make rules about popped bubbles." He jerked his chin in Tenley's direction, the memory washing over him too fast to toss aside. "She used to pop my bubbles so she'd win."

"Did not." Tenley's voice held a smile despite her outward scowl. She cuffed his arm, the touch light as a feather but no less potent than napalm.

She breezed past him, leaving behind the combined scent of horse and the coconut shampoo she'd used for as long as he could remember.

Jade ran around the table and skidded to a stop in front of Tenley.

Mac dragged his gaze away from the unlikely pair and focused on Peter and Margaret. They looked well, older, a bit more worn, but they both smiled at him. Tension knotted in his throat at the glint of something brewing in Peter's eyes. He'd counted the man like a father when his own died during Mac's high school days. Losing Peter after the wedding debacle pained him more than he cared to admit.

Jade twirled, holding out her arms and asking Tenley

to dance. Like the rowdy youth he remembered, Tenley joined in. Joy shone from her face, along with a peacefulness that he'd not seen in years.

Lord, why? Mac staggered over the force of worry gnawing at him. Why him and this awful situation that put him within Tenley's grasp again? She pulled him into her world without even trying.

"Going to be in town for a while?" Peter tapped his fingers on the arms of his wheelchair, keeping time with Tenley's whirling steps.

Mac glanced at Tenley. "Depends."

"On?" Peter pressed, and only his respect for the man kept Mac from saying something he'd regret.

He breathed deep, letting the air expand his lungs, and counted to five. "Got some business to take care of."

Jade and Tenley's laughter rang out clear and strong, and the sound did something to Mac's heart. An ache built, and he pressed a fist to his sternum to keep it contained.

He blinked away the vision threatening to cloud his mind. One where Tenley danced in their kitchen, with their little girl. A dream that would never be realized.

"I think we all know why I'm here. I'd like to not discuss it in her presence." He motioned at Jade but realized that his mood currently included Tenley too.

There had to be a way out of this predicament.

"She'll stay here tonight, and we'll sort everything out once you've had time to digest what's happened." Peter's voice made the order direct and final.

Mac considered arguing when realization dawned. "She knew that we shared custody?" He couldn't say her name out loud. It hurt too much.

Margaret laced her fingers together under her chin and

watched him with a hooded expression. "She found out right after…" Tears filled her eyes and her chin wobbled.

He looked away from the sight of her grief. Margaret and Peter had been like parents to him, Amber, Callie and so many others through the years. They gathered them up like a hen did chicks and gave them a safe place to call home. He'd forever be grateful for their hospitality to him and Amber all those years ago, but he couldn't allow that to cloud his judgment now.

He pushed away from the table. "Jade." The girl spun in his direction, her face wreathed in smiles.

She ran to him, arms wide with the same love and abandon her mother had showed. "Are you staying forever?"

He shook his head once, and her smile morphed into a frown. "I have to leave, but I'll be back tomorrow." Like Peter, Mac made his words into a promise.

He hugged Jade tight and stood.

Tenley fiddled with the edge of her tattered shirt, her mouth flat with disapproval.

Mac escaped to the front porch and patted his leg, indicating Zeus should follow. The dog lay on his back in the dirt path that led from the porch to the driveway. Flowers poked through the ground on either side, evidence of Margaret's love of gardening.

The dog eyed Mac from his upside-down position, tongue lolling out. The pup bounded around Zeus, nipping at his tail and doing his best to get Zeus to engage.

A snort of laughter slipped out before he could stop it. Mac crossed his arms despite the pull and sharp jab of pain in his shoulder. "Don't tell me you like that mangy pup?"

Zeus flipped over and barked. His tail swished in the dirt. It was the most animated movement the dog had made of his own free will since he woke from the surgery that removed a sniper bullet from his side. Maybe Mac's captain was right. Maybe Zeus should be retired. He cuffed a hand over his cheek and strode toward his truck. He'd worry about that problem once he figured out how he was going to raise a little girl all by himself in Chicago.

Chapter Two

❧

The next day, Mac waited outside Leonard's office. At a quarter past nine on a Friday morning, the lawyer's office should be open, but when Mac pulled the door, the lock held fast. He palmed the back of his neck and scoured the street. Shops lined the road on either side, a few of them showing their age with peeling paint and haphazard signs.

Zeus sat at his side, head up and ears pricked forward. Mac put a calming hand on the canine's head. "Easy." Zeus whimpered and looked up, then licked his lips before returning his attention to the shop directly in front of them.

The door to Granny's Diner stood open as a couple exited, allowing tantalizing aromas out into the open air. Mac inhaled, and his stomach rumbled loudly. Through the plate glass windows, he watched people dining and considered abandoning his stakeout for a plate of gravy and biscuits. No one made biscuits and thick, rich gravy like Granny.

Zeus pressed his nose against Mac's leg and let out another whine.

Mac reached into the truck and retrieved Zeus's collapsible bowl and a bottle of water. He poured a healthy portion into the bowl and set it on the sidewalk. While

Zeus lapped at the water, Mac checked the dog's vest. He wasn't actively working, but Zeus's police dog career was long and the vest kept curious people from running up and trying to pet him. Most of the time. Mac kept an eye on the foot traffic moseying up and down the sidewalk. A couple jaywalked a dozen feet away from him, but he paid them no mind. This was Tamarack Springs, proud owner of one stoplight—that almost never worked—and not a single crosswalk. They were more of the throw-your-hand-up-in-thanks-and-jog-across-the-street-while-cars-stopped-for-you kind of town.

Leaving here for Chicago had been a massive culture shock. And now, being back, he scarcely knew where to begin.

Seeing Tenley had hit him harder than he'd expected. He'd put all that behind him years ago. Or so he'd thought. One look. One touch from her, and it all unraveled. All the years apart threatened to collapse and drag him back to when things were good and he felt whole. He picked a flaking paint chip from the side of his truck. He'd lost so much over the years that this, seeing Tenley and knowing nothing could bring back what they had, shouldn't kick him in the gut with enough force to stop his breath.

He'd suffered the loss of his parents, Tenley's love, his wife and now his sister. He and grief were well acquainted. But he still had Jade, and he'd do anything and everything within his power to take care of her. He'd sworn to keep her safe on the day she was born, and he'd uphold that promise. Even if it meant taking her away from Tamarack Springs. From Tenley. The woman he'd given his heart to, only to have it crushed under her boot heel.

Never again.

Tenley didn't deserve the chance to protect Jade. She'd given up that right when she jilted him, proving herself untrustworthy, and all she'd do was end up disappointing him again—or worse, disappointing Jade. He'd suffer if it was just him at risk. But he refused to put Jade through that loss. She loved Tenley. He'd seen it in the way they danced in the kitchen last night.

A stout woman dressed in a paisley apron shuffled out of Granny's. "Malcolm Mitchell, get in here and eat your breakfast." Granny glared at him, her wispy white hair curled in a halo around her head. She brandished a wooden spoon in his direction, eyes eagle-sharp as they raked him over. "Come on. Not telling you twice. Got your food in your booth. And something for the pup too."

Mac opened his mouth.

Granny arched an eyebrow and pointed her spoon at him. "Breakfast is getting cold. Cold gravy never did nobody no good." Old-fashioned Southern charm at its finest, the double negatives thick enough to make even Mac take a moment to appreciate Granny's adept use and the deep drawl that spoke of home.

She yanked the door open with more strength than he thought possible for a woman her age. Granny's Diner had been around longer than Mac had been alive. She was a staple of their little town. Everyone paid attention when Granny spoke, and even though he no longer considered himself part of Tamarack, he knew better than to say no.

He motioned for Zeus and followed her into the diner. Familiar sights, sounds and smells surrounded him. Granny stopped at a table and chatted with the man and woman sitting there before she angled her steps toward the open kitchen behind the long counter. Granny didn't believe in "keeping up with the times" as she called it.

Which meant the diner looked exactly the same as it had when he was a child. Same square tables marching in a line down the center of the diner. Same cracked red coverings on the booths.

"Isaac, get another batch of hash browns ready." Granny slipped behind the counter and disappeared.

Mac's feet moved on instinct, carrying him to a booth left of the door. Sure enough, he found a plate piled high with gravy and biscuits waiting for him, along with a cup of steaming black coffee and a bowl of kibble for Zeus. Mac's brow puckered. How…? Why did Granny have dog food in her diner? He shook his head. The woman was a mystery that no one had ever figured out.

He set the bowl of food on the floor for Zeus and motioned for the dog to eat. Zeus sniffed the bowl before chowing down.

Mac bowed his head, but prayer eluded him. Words tumbled together as though in a race to reach God first, and all he could do was allow his heart to open and let God hear the cry for Himself. Mac grabbed his fork and cut into the flaky biscuit, releasing a puff of steam.

Granny appeared when he reached for the pepper shaker.

He eyed her from the side while shaking pepper onto his sawmill gravy.

She puckered her lips but didn't comment on the blasphemy of seasoning her food before he'd even had a taste. "Who you looking for out there?" She jerked her head toward his green pickup, parked midway between her diner and Leonard's law office.

"Who says I'm looking for anybody?" He eased a bite of piping hot biscuit and gravy into his mouth and sighed as his eyes sank closed. He chewed slowly, relishing the

buttery biscuit and peppery gravy. When he opened his
eyes again, a delighted smile wrinkled Granny's face.

She lowered herself onto the bench seat across from
him, her short stature ensuring he could still see the door
and everyone around him over her head. She gave him a
knowing look that was equal parts annoyance and happiness. "Nobody stands outside my diner, sniffing and pin-
ing but refusing to come inside, unless they're waiting on
somebody mighty important."

Mac ate a second bite while he considered his options.
Most likely half of the town population already knew his
business, but he'd rather not instigate any new rumors.
He sipped his coffee and grinned. "Still serving nothing
but coffee, I see."

Granny harrumphed. "You want water, you go to the
kitchen and get it yourself. Breakfast goes best with coffee." She leaned forward, her smile widening. "And I'm
still smart enough to know when someone's trying to
distract me."

Customers sat all around them, their voices rising and
falling as conversation flowed thick as the honey Granny
bought from Bill, their local beekeeper. Heads turned in
his direction. People he'd known his whole life offered
grins and nods but didn't interrupt. No one interrupted
Granny once she'd taken it upon herself to join someone.

He saw the curiosity, and the knowing.

"Point taken." Mac took another sip and waited for a
woman carrying a full breakfast platter to pass by his
booth. Once she was out of earshot, he spoke. "What time
does Leonard come to work?"

"That old coot?" Granny tipped her head back and
laughter rolled out. Her shoulders shook. "Honey, you're

better off looking for him at home than at the office. Old Leonard don't come in unless it's an emergency."

"I see." Mac resumed his breakfast, though the biscuits now sat hard as lumps of coal in his gut. The flavor though, the flavor made it worthwhile. Had he considered it an emergency when he couldn't get hold of Mac? Was that why Jade stayed at the ranch with Tenley? After Mac's abrupt departure from the office yesterday, Leonard was probably more than happy to wash his hands of Mac and Tenley's predicament.

Shared guardianship. The words tasted sour in his mouth and turned him away from the rest of his breakfast. Pushing the plate aside, he wrapped both hands around the coffee cup and leaned his elbows on the table. "Guess I'll need his phone number. Or address."

Granny snorted. "Thought you were smarter than that, Mac." The use of his nickname softened the anger curling his stomach into a tight knot. Granny leaned across the table and patted his forearm. "Sorry about your sister. Know it doesn't help but can't let you get out of here without saying it anyway. She was a delightful girl. Came in every Saturday morning for breakfast. The three of them." She met his gaze, her own full of grief. "Take care of that girl."

"I will." He forced his throat to work, to push the words into existence and will them into truth. Jade was all that he had left in this world. He couldn't lose her too.

Zeus poked his nose into Mac's leg, his whine drawing attention.

Mac ruffled the upright ears and rolled his shoulders to loosen the tension. He'd almost lost Zeus to a bullet, and now might lose him to retirement. He didn't want to start over with another canine partner. Or another human one, if he was being honest. Pain sliced through his shoulder when he shifted, reminding him of that night. Of all the things he'd done wrong, all to save his partner's life, and he'd gotten both Zeus and himself shot in the process. His captain used the injury to put Mac on administrative leave without making it obvious. Mac broke protocol that night, and almost seven years of playing by the book didn't undo this one night where it all went sideways.

"You still with me?" Granny peered at him over the rim of her glasses.

Mac released his death grip on the coffee cup and resumed patting Zeus, who'd begun inching toward Granny.

She looked at Zeus, then at Mac. "That dog of yours looks almighty worn out."

He felt the statement all the way to his bones.

"Seems his owner is too," she continued.

"Zeus isn't mine." Mac drained the coffee. "I'm a K-9 handler in Chicago. Zeus and I work together."

Granny harrumphed. "Honey, I'd love to be a fly on the wall the day you try and tell him that. Better yet, I want to watch if anyone is ever fool enough to try and take him away from you. Don't care what your job is. That dog is yours. He's accepted you as his human. End of story."

Mac glanced at Zeus, who stared back at him with that searching look. It was true. Zeus hadn't connected with any of the other K-9 officers until Mac. He'd been on the verge of early retirement since he refused to follow orders. It had taken Mac a week to earn the dog's trust, and they'd been inseparable since. He followed all the rules about keeping Zeus. He wasn't a pet. He wasn't a family dog. He was a working partner. Something Laura and he had argued over more than once. She'd wanted to make a pet out of Zeus, but Mac had stood firm.

His thoughts turned foul, and he heaved them into the darkest corner of his mind before they took root and grew. "Thanks for dragging me in for breakfast." He changed the conversation without bothering to sugarcoat his rush to leave.

Granny narrowed her eyes at him. "Why don't I let Leonard know you need to see him? He'll be at church Sunday. You can talk to him then."

Mac ignored the built-in insinuation that he'd even go to church. He grabbed Zeus's leash and stood. "Monday morning is soon enough. Tell him I'll be waiting at 8:00 a.m." He slid two twenties under the edge of his plate.

"You take that money and put it to good use." Granny poked a finger at him.

Mac grinned back. "I just did." He sauntered away, feeling lighter now that he had a plan in motion. Monday morning, he and Leonard would sit down and iron out all the wrinkles Amber's will left behind. In the meantime, he needed to get back to Jade. He'd promised to come back, and he'd keep his word, even if it meant seeing Tenley.

Tenley turned a slow circle, keeping Jade and Freckles front and center in her line of sight. "Good, Jade. Keep him moving forward. Use pressure from your knees. Good."

Jade's grin broke through like the sunshine after a rainstorm. It overtook the clouds that had become the girl's expression for far too long. Not that Tenley blamed her. Jade had every right to scowl and grieve and want to lie in bed all day with her stuffed animals. But Tenley didn't deny the burst of joy singing through her heart at the sight of that proud smile.

Freckles continued his steady walk around the corral. He'd been trained to listen to voice commands but also to feel for his rider's wants through the reins and leg cues. Right now, Tenley wanted horse and rider to work together. Jade was an established rider, and knew how to guide her mount even at her young age.

Jade sat easy in the saddle, the reins relaxed in her hands and her feet firmly in the stirrups. She stared ahead, her body language letting Freckles know which way she wanted to go. "Can I ride with the class tomorrow?" Jade cast a look at Tenley, then looked ahead again.

"Sure." Tenley kept turning. Her hat brim shielded her from the worst of the sun's glare but reminded her yet again of how nice it would be to have a covered arena like the one at Daniel Wells's riding school. She tried not to feel inadequate with her single arena and barn. Tried to stuff the jealousy down. Daniel would offer the use of his arena in a heartbeat if she asked. Not that she ever would. This was her dream, and she'd accomplish it her way, on her terms.

Enough of that. She sounded like her brother Brody.

Boots scuffed nearby. Goose bumps prickled the back of her neck, and she knew who stood at the rail behind her without turning around. Mac. He'd come back, just like he'd said he would. Good ole Mac. Reliable as the day was long. Never backed down from what he believed was right. Willing to jump into any mess for those he loved when they needed saving. And always true to his word.

Spots danced in front of Tenley's eyes, a harsh reminder to stop holding her breath. She gulped air and tried not to shiver when his gaze landed between her shoulder blades with the intensity of a laser. No one else ever made her feel this way.

Jade rode toward Mac, forcing Tenley to turn. She did,

as slow as possible, while wrangling her face into anything other than the regret that bubbled up in his presence. He deserved an apology for what she'd done. To him. To them. He deserved the truth. A truth that he'd asked her family for when Tenley disappeared. But her shame trapped her, and Mac knowing the real reason for their failed wedding felt like it would tip her over the edge of an unscalable chasm. So, they'd stood by her request not to tell him about the alcoholism, and he'd hightailed it out of her life—probably as hurt and confused by the blockade erected from Mom, Dad and Brody, people he counted as family—before she had a chance to come to terms with her overnight stint in jail and subsequent months in rehab.

Barking erupted from the barn, and a ball of white fur bounded toward the corral.

Tenley groaned in time with the puppy's playful yips.

Mac looked over his shoulder, giving Tenley a reprieve.

"Rascal." Jade called the puppy, her tone scolding even though she laughed.

The puppy hurtled toward Freckles, darting under the fence's lower railing and giving Tenley a wide berth like he knew she'd keep him from reaching the horse.

"Get that dog out of there." Mac's voice shook, and Tenley didn't know which was heavier, the anger or the fear.

Jade and Freckles kept moving forward. Rascal raced around Freckles, pretending to nip at his fetlocks. His teeth snapped together on Freckles' tail.

Mac hissed through his teeth and squeezed between the rails. He ran toward Jade, face set and jaw tight. "Why aren't you doing anything?" He glared at Tenley as he raced past. "I knew this would happen. You never think, Tenley."

What? Her spine snapped into a straight line and her hands landed on her hips. "Freckles, stop." The gelding halted in his tracks.

Mac didn't pause his headlong rush toward Jade.

Jade frowned. "Why'd you stop him?"

Mac yanked Jade from the saddle amid her protests and held her tight. "I can't believe you'd put her in danger."

"Jade, go put your dog in the stall. Like I told you to do before the lesson started." Tenley matched Mac, glare for glare. "While I explain to your uncle why he should never, ever enter my arena and approach the horses without my permission."

Jade wiggled. "Put me down, Uncle Mac."

Rascal never stopped bouncing. He zoomed past Mac, ran under Freckles' belly, and back out of the corral.

Mac lowered Jade to the ground, but he kept hold of her like he might snatch her up and run away at any second. His fear made no sense. Mac grew up here, riding the same horses she'd ridden. He knew Tenley would never put a child in danger. Didn't he?

Jade sighed, the sound older than a girl her age should know how to make. "I did put him in the stall. I promise I did."

"He must have dug his way out. Again." Tenley resisted the urge to rush into an explanation. "Go on. See if you can catch him."

"That dog—"

"Wait." Tenley interrupted Mac. She jutted her chin toward Jade. The girl let out a groan and trotted off after the pup. Tenley rounded on Mac. "In what world do you think it's okay to come in here, interrupt my lesson and jerk Jade around like she's a rag doll?"

Fury rolled through her, and a matching look seared

her from the depths of Mac's brown eyes. He took a step forward. "In what world do you allow that little girl on a horse while a dog runs around out of control?"

Tenley sank her teeth into her cheek to keep from blasting him with the harshest words that came to mind. She paused long enough to cleanse her thoughts and lowered her hands to her pockets. "I'm going to say this once, out of respect for you and your role as Jade's co-guardian. Freckles is a therapy horse. He's been trained to deal with any and every situation with one reaction. Nothing."

"You're not putting Jade's life in danger on someone else's word." Mac all but crackled with the furious anger drawing his eyes into narrow slits.

"It's my word, Mac, mine. Not someone else's."

Mac splayed his hands in a so-what motion, and Tenley swallowed her retort. He'd never listen. Her words and promises meant nothing to him, not after what she did.

She could tell him all day how many hours she'd put into verifying Freckles'—and all the other horses'—ability to handle any situation. Time Mac would never give her. Not that it would matter. But maybe if he took half a second to stop panicking and focus, he'd know that for himself. She also didn't have time to delve into why Mac was panicking in the first place.

She motioned at the gelding standing still as a stone and took a step toward Mac with more bravado than she felt. "And I'll say this once as well. Never talk to me that way again. I don't care if you hate me. Don't ever speak that way in front of Jade. I may not deserve your love or forgiveness, or even your respect, but you won't force your prejudices on to Jade."

Mac's jaw could smash concrete into submission. When he ducked his head, his gaze pulling away from hers, she forced herself back into his line of sight. "I promised Amber that I'd take care of Jade. That means something. Whether you believe it or not," she said.

He inhaled deeply, no doubt brewing up a storm of arguments. Before he could utter a word, Jade loped back into the corral with Rascal in her arms. "Uncle Mac, will you help me train Rascal? You know about dogs, right?"

He shook his head and took a step away from Tenley. She noted the sudden haggardness in his eyes and the way he continually rubbed his shoulder while wincing.

"Wait." She didn't mean to plead and stopped before she said more. One word. A single syllable, but it stretched across the years separating them and offered the tentative bridge of hope she desperately needed. From the looks of Mac, he needed it too. She used to be able to read him. Way back when, she'd have known in half a second what he was thinking. Not anymore. He'd learned how to guard himself against her.

Her stomach lurched and tightened. She'd loved him more than she thought possible. Or healthy. What he considered the ultimate betrayal she knew to be the only way to set him free from a lifetime of regret. Regret he had no idea he'd managed to avoid.

Jade grunted at Rascal's weight and lowered the pup to the dusty ground. "Uncle Mac?"

He spun to face Jade, his last look at Tenley full of all the things they'd never said. A breath hissed between his teeth when he dropped to a knee, bringing himself to Jade's level. "Of course, I'll help you train your puppy."

While Jade grinned and hugged Mac, he glared at Tenley over his shoulder.

Jade pulled away. "I'll go put him up, then you can watch the rest of my class." Her nose wrinkled. "That's okay, right, Aunt Tenley? Long as he doesn't come into the corral again?" she said respectfully.

"That's fine." She answered before Mac could say a word.

He faced her once Jade walked out of earshot. "She's not going to keep riding."

"You try telling her that. Freckles is part of Jade's equine therapy program. The grief counselor from the Department of Family and Children Services recommended it, and she signs off on all Jade's paperwork. You'll have to take it up with her." Tenley shrugged even though her heart drummed hard and fast.

Mac ripped off the ball cap covering his dark hair and scrubbed a hand over his scalp. "Fine. Then, she's not allowed to ride unless I'm here."

Tenley couldn't help it. A bark of laughter shot out. She crossed her arms. "She rides when she's scheduled to ride. If you want to be here, that's fine. I'll give you a copy of her riding times once we're finished here." She held up a hand. "But if you're not here, that's on you. She rides anyway. I'm not responsible for you."

"Yeah, you washed your hands of that a long time ago." Mac's voice lowered to a growl. His expression was drawn tight, lines fanning out from his eyes and narrowing them to slits. "If you have something to say to me, say it now. Get it over with."

"Oh, there's plenty I want to say to you, but not here. Not now. I have a class to teach." She stalked over to Freckles and gathered up the gelding's reins. The horse followed her to the mounting block near the gate. Tenley spoke to Mac over her shoulder. "Right now, you need to get on the other side of the fence."

"And if I don't?" He dared to lean against the railing and cross his arms.

Tenley gripped the reins until her fingers cramped. What could she do to convince him? "You're not qualified personnel."

"So, if I'm in here, then Jade can't ride?" He smirked and crossed his arms. "I think I'll stay."

"What happened to you?" The question shot out before she could stop it. "Where's the uncle that Jade always talks about? The one who promised to take her on a trail ride the next time he was in town?"

Mac reeled back like she'd struck him. He pushed off from the rail and palmed open the gate without saying a single word.

Jade walked out of the barn, and they both went silent.

Tenley regretted trying to break into Mac's past. She kept an eye on him while Jade hopped in the saddle. Mac had lost so many people in his life. Their names flashed through her mind. She hesitated on one. Laura. His wife.

It surprised her that Mac had fallen in love so soon after leaving. Amber had been sure that Mac still loved Tenley, but Tenley had known better. Tenley had felt immeasurable grief when she heard of Laura's passing. With Amber gone, Mac was alone except for Jade. She didn't blame him for wanting to cling tight to his last thread of family.

For the remainder of the class, he stood with his arms atop the rail and a deepening scowl pulling lines from his mouth.

Tenley did her best to ignore him, but it was like trying to ignore an approaching storm. The small hairs on the back of her neck prickled. She could all but smell the burnt ozone coming from the lightning strikes Mac sent her way.

It took enormous effort to keep her body relaxed and her tone even, but she managed. *Lord, help me get through this.* She tried to hold on to the sliver of peace the prayer offered, but it eluded her. Mac coming back into her life churned up the past she'd tried so hard to bury.

Chapter Three

Tenley let a breath of relief escape when the time came for class to start and Mac hadn't arrived to hover, but then she felt bad for Jade, who continually scanned the arena and whose little shoulders deflated when it became obvious he wasn't coming.

Tenley waved at her two additional instructors. Carl and Julie had come highly recommended, and Tenley loved working with the married duo. She also loved Saturday classes when all the kids rode together.

Carl nudged his hat up with his thumb and glanced at his watch. "Ready when you are, boss."

Tenley swallowed the lump of disappointment she told herself was for Jade and clapped her hands. It was ironic that she'd wrought such turmoil in Mac's life, and here she was mooning over him. She didn't deserve a second chance, even if her subconscious quietly hoped for it. Still, seeing him stirred up old embers she thought had gone cold.

She gave herself a little shake. Back to business. "Alright, we'll begin with a walk. Jasmine will lead today. Jas, stop at the gate after the third round. Okay?"

"Got it." The girl bobbed her head. Being the leader was a privilege that changed every class. Today was Jasmine's first time, and from the way she sat up straight in the saddle, she planned on taking it seriously.

Her class of six kids sat quietly while she stepped between Carl and Julie.

Cody, a scrappy tow-headed boy who was also one of the younger kids in the group, was here for grief counseling like Jade. His dad had pulled Tenley aside upon their arrival to mention Cody's anxiety had improved though his grief ebbed and flowed. Cody leaned forward and patted his horse's neck. She was one of the tallest horses they stabled, and even though little Cody looked outmatched on her, Tenley had her reasons for the pairing. The gray mare didn't move, standing as she'd been trained until given the signal.

"Lead on, Jasmine." Tenley lifted her hand and let it fall.

Jasmine nudged her horse into a slow walk. The others moved one by one, falling into a line, one horse length between each horse. Smiles broke out, a sight Tenley never tired of. She could watch kids ride all day every day, and each time they broke through whatever trauma or distress that made them feel trapped, she knew she'd made the right choice in opening an equine therapy center here on the ranch.

She turned on her heel, keeping her kids in sight. The small, covered arena wasn't as nice as the one at Wells Riding Academy, but it worked for Tenley and her groups. Someday, she'd expand.

Jasmine continued her slow walk, her horse's sorrel coat contrasting with the white fence behind the mare. Parents sat in a row of bleachers near the gate where the riders mounted and dismounted. The barn connected to the covered arena via a short, roofed path that led straight to the gate and gave the riders a feeling of freedom while also maintaining safety.

"Good job, Cody." Tenley praised the young boy when he gently nudged his horse back in line after the mare weaved closer to the rail than the others. She lost her footing a little, but Cody didn't overreact. He'd started out so afraid, but now he handled her with skill and more confidence—well, most of the time anyway.

"Tenley." Mac's voice brought her head around, distracting her. He yelled her name a second time and motioned for her to join him. He waved a set of papers at her like they were on fire, and she had to take them or he'd get burned.

The nerve.

She shook her head in a negative motion. Now wasn't the time. "You're doing great, kids."

That's when she saw silent tears running down Cody's face. She'd been about to join Mac to put him in his place, and almost missed them.

Tenley frowned and walked toward the little boy and his big horse. "Everything okay, Cody?"

The boy nodded, but his chin wobbled and he clutched the reins in both fists. "I don't want to stop. I want to keep going, but I'm afraid."

She kept pace with him. "It's okay. Can I walk with you? You can keep going. I'll be right here."

He sniffled and nodded. "Yeah."

Losing his mom at his age had turned the once-confident boy into the anxious quiet one before her. It was a normal grief reaction for such a young child, and one they could help him work through. His happy self was still in there, but grief made him afraid. Learning to ride a muscled, tall mount like Tank, along with regular counseling sessions, was helping him overcome some of those fears.

"Nice and easy. Let's keep it at a walk for a few more laps. Can you tell me what's making you afraid?"

"I... I think she might buck me off. I don't want to fall." Little sobs escaped. *The wobble earlier at the fence, that's what did it*, Tenley thought. She'd turn it into a lesson. His mother had died from a fall, though not from a horse.

"Has Tank ever bucked before?"

"Uh-uh." His head shook.

"You've been to class, what, five times? Has Tank always been gentle? Have you always been safe on her?"

"Mmm-hmm," he said, seeing where this was going.

"I think Tank hit her hoof earlier. Like when you stub your toe. When you trip over your feet, does it make you mad?" Tenley made her best mean face.

Cody giggled, "No!"

"So is your thought a good, helpful thought or a bad, unhelpful thought?"

"Bad!" he yelled, getting excited.

Tenley matched his pitch. "And what do we do with those bad thoughts?"

"We flush them down the toilet!" It wasn't exactly a horse analogy, but the kids didn't care. The other students shouted it with him again, this time louder, and they all laughed.

Mac watched with quiet curiosity, and put aside the bundle of papers.

Some of the tension bled out of his expression as they passed him, one of the kids cracking a potty joke that had nothing to do with therapy. Mac lowered his hands to his hips and gripped his belt. He tried to hide the ghost of a smile creeping free. He wore jeans and another T-shirt with what looked to be a pair of brand-new cowboy boots.

The soft brown gleamed in contrast to her own battered and scarred boots.

She motioned for Julie to take over when she thought Cody was okay, then made the slow trek over to a waiting Mac.

Memories shot through Tenley. Images of Mac in his sheriff's deputy uniform right after he'd completed his training flashed through her mind. He'd stood just like that. Tall and proud, gripping the belt like a rodeo champion would a prize buckle. Smiling that same smile. The full one though. A lot of hard work went into earning the right to strap the utility belt on.

She looked over at the kids, finding healing in her therapy school. Tenley's throat worked as tension gathered in her shoulders and pressed down on her heart. This school wouldn't have existed. And all his hard work wouldn't have meant a thing if they'd gotten married. Maybe she wouldn't have gotten help. Maybe her next accident would have been her last one. Maybe her arrest would have stalled his career if anyone ever found out a deputy's wife was an inebriated road hazard?

She'd spent weeks coming to terms with her problems and the potential fallout of a deputy's wife getting arrested. Didn't matter what for or that it happened before the wedding. Tamarack Springs had a long memory when it came to juicy gossip. But her downfall had happened in Bridgeport, far enough away from their sleepy little town's gossip mill. Still, she was afraid her problem would follow her back then.

So many what-ifs, and here he was, stirring them up like horses swatting flies with swishing tails.

Behind her, her co-leaders directed the group back to

dismount. Class was over already? With Mac watching, everything sped up double time.

Jade had beat the group to the punch though. She'd already dismounted and removed her saddle. She called to Mac while rushing toward the tack room. "I'm almost done. We can train Rascal together."

The look Mac gave Tenley said he'd rather be doing anything other than working with that rambunctious pup, but he didn't argue. A promise was a promise, to Mac.

Tenley grimaced.

"Where's Zeus?" She'd meant to ask the day before but lost track of the question after their argument.

"He's at the house with your parents." Mac lifted one eyebrow. "Didn't want him down here getting into trouble around the horses like that pup."

"I'm sure he'd be fine." Tenley shrugged.

Mac laughed, the sound cold and cruel. "You would think that. Troublesome Tenley." The old nickname shot out of his mouth like a snake spitting venom. "Always thinking that everything will work out. Never prepared for reality."

She snapped her teeth together with a click, trapping angry words behind them. How dare he? They both knew the casualties that came with living. Her father's accident was the single worst thing that she'd ever experienced aside from leaving Mac. He used her moniker as a weapon, knowing she despised it. Yes, she'd been the one always getting into trouble as a kid. She claimed middle-child syndrome, though there was more to it than that.

It wasn't like Mac to be cruel. Even if she deserved it.

"What happened to you?" She asked the same question from the day before. He'd changed so much more than she'd anticipated. Gone was the funny and lighthearted man who'd stolen her heart. In his place was this jaded and cynical person she hardly recognized.

"I grew up." Mac thrust the papers he'd been cradling at her, like they were a bomb. "And I brought these."

Granted, Mac knew printing the "Voluntary Surrender of Rights" form from an internet lawyer's website was a risk, but one he was willing to take. Getting ahold of old Leonard to do the deed himself was a harder task than running down a drug dealer—in hiding—on purpose. It made him wonder if the old lawyer had something to hide, or some nefarious matchmaking plan concocted by Granny, or if it was just that the man was so old he spent more time napping than working these days.

Now, if he could only get Tenley to sign it and be done so he could get back to Chicago—with a six-year-old. He swallowed the lump forming in his throat and ran a hand down his face. Calling Tenley *troublesome* wasn't going to help his case, but she was a burr in his side that he couldn't help scratching hard.

Tenley eyed the papers, her eyes snapping fire at him. She took a giant step back. "I'm not signing that."

"It's what's best for Jade." Mac hit her with a low blow, and he knew it. He had to try. He'd done enough waiting for Tenley. "I'm done here. Sign the papers and let me take Jade home."

Tenley's expression morphed so quick he almost missed it as she hid her anger between one blink and the next. She closed the distance. "Jade is home." She jerked her head toward the barn. "And she'll be headed this way in about three minutes, so you'd better put those away and get ready to train that dog."

Mac was the one who could use some training. Or a

crash course in raising a little girl. How was he supposed to do this? He folded the papers and thrust them in Tenley's direction. "You know this is what's best." He pushed because that's what he was good at. He'd built a career on being the guy who followed the letter of the law. He never wavered. Never backed down. He'd beat this thing with Tenley if it took every last breath. Breath that grew shorter the longer she stared at him without moving.

"I'm not a criminal you can scare into doing what you want." She crossed her arms and took another step closer. If not for the fence between them, she'd probably have tried to haul him away. "I have Jade's best interests at heart. You're just anxious to get away from me, and you'll end up hurting Jade because you can't stand the heat." She dared him to contradict her.

Mac swallowed the first retort that came to mind. Even Tenley didn't deserve to have those words thrown at her. She was right. He was running scared and trying to drag Jade along for the ride.

Tenley was a contradiction to the woman he used to know. Still bold and full of fire, but this one had a tenacity and grit that he'd only seen in people who'd suffered.

What experience did Tenley have with grief and agony?

Tenley moved with lightning speed. She snatched the papers from his hand and ripped them to shreds then threw the pieces into the air.

Mac watched the bits flutter in the breeze until they landed on the ground and lay still.

"I will do everything in my power to protect her." Mac stooped, ready to duck under the rail and gather the scraps. "Jade is the last of my family. She's everything to me."

Tenley flinched like the words were a physical blow he'd dealt her.

Tough. He had every right to say the truth.

Childish laughter spilled out from behind Mac. He straightened. "Jade doesn't need to know about this."

"Of course." Tenley spat the words at him. "I'm not the one trying to ruin her life by taking her away from everything—and everyone—she knows and loves."

That's not what he was doing.

Jade skipped toward him, hand in hand with Cody, the little boy who'd been struggling earlier.

Tenley wore a smile bright as sunshine. The sight pinched and poked at Mac. She'd make a great mother. The kind of mother he'd wanted for his kids. Now those dreams were shot to bits no bigger than the pieces of paper Tenley had left behind.

Chapter Four

Tenley couldn't believe Mac's audacity. If Jade hadn't interrupted, she might have tossed her cowgirl hat at his feet and showed him what her boot spurs could do—if he didn't run away fast enough.

Lord help me, she prayed, and took a deep calming breath. *Lord, help me show Mac that I've changed. For his own sake, not mine. Let him see the damage he could do to Jade by taking her away. And if it's better for Jade to leave, then help me see that as Your will.*

Jade tucked her small hand into Mac's giant one and grinned up at him. Her grin faltered, no doubt feeling the tension, and she looked back at Tenley with such anguish that Tenley's heart broke into a thousand little pieces.

"You ready, Uncle Mac?" she said quietly. "Rascal is at Molly's with Luke."

Mac's steps hesitated when Tenley started walking with them. "I don't need help training the dog." The words were halting, almost like he didn't quite mean them.

"Didn't offer any. You demanded to watch Jade ride, I demand to watch you train Rascal." She infused strength into her spine and strode alongside. Two could play this game he'd made up with rules no one else understood.

Tenley hung back while Mac and Jade approached her

sister Molly's house. The log cabin–style home shone with love and attention. The front porch was swept clean and the windows sparkled.

Jade thundered up the steps and banged her fist on the door. "Luke, come on. We're going to train Rascal."

The door burst open. Five-year-old Luke and Rascal spilled out onto the porch in a tumble of arms and legs. Luke's dark blond hair stuck up in every direction. He rolled to his feet and grabbed Rascal's collar before the pup took a nosedive down the steps.

"Grab his leash." Mac's shoulders shook with what appeared to be repressed laughter.

Luke's nose scrunched as he frowned. His freckles shone bright in the sunlight, the adorableness diminishing his growing scowl. "Who're you?"

"Luke." Molly admonished her son from the open doorway. Wisps of hair that matched Luke's fanned around her face. Red splotches covered her cheeks, a sure indication she'd been baking. Molly wiped her hands on a dishcloth. Her gaze skipped over Mac, then came back to rest on him. Her mouth opened in a vivid display of shock. "First, Callie. Now you. Which other long-lost residents will come back next?"

She didn't seem to want an answer to her question, so Tenley didn't offer one. Her sister had a point. Callie had come back after ten years. Mac after almost seven. Tamarack Springs hadn't seen this many prodigals returning in its whole history as a town.

That adage "you can never go home again" had been true for a long time, but Tenley understood that anyone could come back from the darkness. If she could, then anything was possible.

Jade joined Luke, the two of them wrestling with Rascal. "What do we do first?" Jade held the wriggling puppy with both hands around his middle.

Molly passed Luke a leash, which the boy clipped to the collar. Mac took the leash from Luke and the dog from Jade. "First, let's get some of this energy out."

"Never going to happen," Tenley whispered under her breath.

"I heard that." Mac grinned as he passed, then seemed to remember who he was talking to. He paused, and for a fraction of a second, he looked like he might apologize.

Tenley moved out of the way, then fell in line behind the kids when Mac moved on. They walked in Mac's footprints, laughing and falling into each other when his strides lengthened and they couldn't keep up.

Jade giggled. "You walk too big." She leaped from one step to the next but lost her balance on the landing and tumbled to the side.

Mac turned around in time to see what they were doing. He paled enough that Tenley almost reached out a hand to steady him.

Rascal chose that moment to leap from Mac's arms and pounce on Jade. He licked her face and wiggled all over, his tail fanning the dirt track Mac followed, which led from Molly's house to their parents' house.

Mac dropped into a crouch and helped Jade sit up. Luke mimicked Mac's posture, and his scowl.

"How long have you had this dog?" Mac zeroed in on Tenley.

She met him look for look. "Couple weeks."

"Have you taught him anything?" The look he gave her—well, she'd seen it before. The accusations in Mac's glare were far too memorable.

Everything that came from the man's mouth had bite.

Was there anything left of the old Mac inside? Sadness swamped her, and she forced down the automatic, inflammatory response. She was not the same girl he thought he knew. She'd grown up, matured. Yes, the Troublesome Tenley nickname stuck around tighter than burrs in a horse's tail, but she was handling it. She could handle this too. And honestly, she was sad for him "No. I haven't had time."

"You don't get a dog if you don't have time to train it properly."

Tenley gave a hunch of her shoulders.

"Don't be mad." Jade threw herself at Mac's back and wrapped her arms around his neck. "I begged and begged. Cried too."

Mac rocked forward with a grunt and a wince. His breath came in short bursts and sweat broke out along his jaw. He was in pain. Concern bolted through Tenley, and it was all she could do not to throw herself on the ground beside him and offer to help. He wouldn't appreciate her interference though. Even before the wedding fiasco, Mac never knew how to ask for help. He had that in common with her and her siblings.

Rascal barked and bounced high enough to lick Mac's chin. He nudged the dog aside and patted Jade's leg. "I'm not mad."

Jade waited several seconds before she slid from his back. "If you're not mad, then you can go trail riding with us tomorrow." She skipped around in front of Mac.

"I can't."

"You promised." Jade's green eyes sparked with enough fire that even Mac seemed taken aback. "Last time in Chicago, you said you'd ride with me the next time you were here. You're here. Now you ride." Tiny arms crossed and her jaw stuck out in a mirror image of her mother, frankly with a whole lot of Mac too. It took Tenley's breath.

Mac's jaw worked side to side. He looked at Tenley, probably hoping she'd refuse to let him go. She held up her hands in a show of surrender. "This is between you two. You made that promise. Not me." And they both knew not to trust her promises. Or Mac thought he did, based on the way his eyes sought hers before skipping away. But Mac's promises were usually a sure thing.

"Okay. Alright." He ruffled Jade's hair. "I'll go trail riding with you."

Mac approached his sister's house the same way he'd enter an interrogation room. Shoulders back, chin up. He all but dared the house to offer the slightest hint of a confrontation when all he wanted was a confession. Silly, really, considering it was just a house. He motioned for Zeus to sit at the bottom step and waited for the dog to follow through before he put his boot on the pressure-treated wood.

He couldn't believe she was gone.

The two-bedroom ranch home glared back at him, challenging him through twin windows on either side of the front door. He stomped across the leaf-littered porch and twisted the knob. Locked. He took a step back and tipped over one of the empty flower planters while craning his head around in search of a key. Surely Amber had left a spare somewhere. She was always forgetting hers since she and Zack almost never bothered locking the door at all.

It was the only thing they'd ever argued about as adults. Every time she came to visit him in Chicago, he brought up the house, and she called him out for letting Chicago ruin his memories of small-town life.

No one in Tamarack Springs had been robbed for as long as Mac could remember. Didn't matter. That one-in-a-million chance was enough to drive him to distraction. Their tiny town also hadn't suffered a major vehicle accident since Tenley's father was involved in a hit-and-run nearly eleven years ago either. Didn't stop his sister and her husband from a fatal crash.

Stop. Just…stop. Mac gripped the concrete flower pot with both hands and forced out a breath. Spending the morning helping Jade with her pup had loosened the knots and let him breathe freely for the first time in months. He treasured those moments, every second spent with his precious niece. The thought of taking her away from here ate at him night and day, but what choice did he have? His life, his career, everything was in Chicago. Not to mention the sight of Tenley threatened to knock him to his knees.

The *whoop-whoop* of a police siren dragged Mac's attention away from the front door. He spun around and watched as the police car rolled up in Amber's driveway. The white-and-black sheriff's vehicle stood out in the overgrown grass.

Mac moved down the steps, out of the shadows and into the sunlight peppering the ground, turning the trees golden. He kept his hands within sight and his body relaxed.

"Well, I'll be." Sheriff Dodge Hanks opened the car door and smacked his palm on the open window. "I knew it. I told Martha there weren't no way somebody'd try to break into this place. Minute I heard you were back in town, I knew it was you." He unfolded his lanky frame from the car and stood to his full height. Gray threaded through the dark brown hair, and lines creased the sheriff's cheeks. The years had made quite a difference.

Mac didn't bother keeping back a smile. He covered the ground between them and held out a hand. "Sheriff. Good to see you."

The sheriff shook Mac's hand, his grip as strong as ever. "Been a long time, son."

Mac felt the years unspool. This man had taught him everything he knew about police work. Had given him a place within the department without hesitation and helped Mac learn the ropes. Then, when things fell apart with Tenley, the sheriff hadn't batted an eye when Mac said he needed to leave. That he couldn't stay in the same town, seeing her day after day.

It was the sheriff's recommendation that got Mac's foot in the door in a small precinct in Chicago. He'd earned his way from there.

And now they'd come full circle. Mac let his hands fall to his sides and eyed the house over his shoulder. "Just came by to check on things."

"Yeah? Not moving in?" Sheriff Hanks scrubbed one knuckle over his cheek. "Well, suppose that might be tough, but what with you caring for little Jade, I thought you might not want to sell."

Mac's entire body stiffened. His pulse was a rabid thing, racing and erratic. "What are you talking about?"

"Huh?" Sheriff Hanks stared at Mac.

Zeus barked, and both men looked over.

The tension bled out of Mac, and he snapped his fingers. "Zeus, come."

"The mighty Zeus." Sheriff Hanks whistled appreciatively. "Heard a lot about him. How's he doing since the accident?"

"Is that what they're calling it?" Mac snorted a laugh.

Sheriff Hanks's expression didn't change, but a muscle ticked twice in his jaw. "You'd call it something else?"

"Yeah. I call it a rookie move made by a seasoned cop who knew better than to break protocol." He paced up and down the sidewalk. "I knew better. I knew what to do but ignored the rules."

"You saved your partner's life," Hanks said. A breeze rippled through the oak tree leafed out in the front yard. Its limbs rattled together as though in agreement.

"He never should've been in danger." Mac grabbed Zeus's collar when the dog paced alongside him. Soulful eyes locked on to Mac, and Zeus pressed in tight to Mac's leg. He'd gone into protection mode, sensing Mac's distress, and was doing his best to figure out what it was that Mac needed.

Sheriff Hanks put a hand on Mac's shoulder, stilling his furious steps. Zeus shoved his body between Hanks and Mac until Hanks lowered his arm. "Son, I understand your frustration. You did a decent thing, and you and your dog were shot. You did what you thought was right in the moment to save a man's life. There's no wrong in that."

"I missed my sister's funeral." He hadn't meant to say that, but being here, at her house with memories falling through him faster and faster, they refused to be denied. "I should have been here. Jade needed me."

The world closed in around him, suffocating. It was all too much.

He had to get away. He had to figure out how to get Jade away from Tenley's guardianship and get her back to Chicago where he could protect her. He was *not* going to lose someone else he loved.

"You're here now. Make the most of it." Sheriff Hanks

waved toward Amber's house. "And now that you own this place, maybe stay awhile. Get your bearings back. Taking a shot like that does things to a man." He brushed a hand across his abdomen, and Mac remembered that Hanks had been shot years ago in a situation much like Mac experienced. If anyone understood, Hanks did.

Mac finally realized what else Hanks said. "What do you mean, I own this house?"

"Leonard didn't tell you? That old coot. We need a new lawyer in town." Sheriff Hanks scooped his black ball cap from his head and ruffled his graying hair. "All this confusion with Jade would never have snowballed if the man could still make it through a single court case without falling asleep. Guess the cat's out of the bag now though. No sense trying to put it back in." He heaved a breath and replaced the cap. "Amber left this place to you. Her husband had no family, so it seemed like the logical thing to do. Mortgage insurance paid off the deed free and clear. Least, that's what I heard from Leonard. The man still knows how to gossip, I guess."

Was everyone talking about his sister's life and death? A raw mixture of hurt and betrayal threatened to overwhelm him.

"No." The denial came immediately, without his thinking about it. He did not need one more thing trying to keep him here in Tamarack Springs.

Sheriff Hanks cocked his head to the side. "I suppose now's not the right time to tell you that I'd love to have you back in my department?"

Mac took a step back and held up both hands. Zeus followed Mac's lead, walking backward but keeping his body between Mac and Hanks.

"Definitely not." Mac forced everything down. He

couldn't think. Couldn't breathe. Things were coming at him from every angle. He had no place to go that felt safe.

Least of which his dead sister's home.

Chapter Five

Tenley managed to keep it together through church and the ride back to the ranch on Sunday morning. Jade chattered from the back seat, her voice rising and falling in equal parts. The one-sided conversation consisted mostly of Jade's excitement over Mac coming to ride with them today. Tenley sank her nails into the steering wheel as her pulse skittered quicker than a nervous colt.

The man had been gone nearly seven years, and she couldn't spend a single day without him by her side.

She'd love to sidestep this whole day. Or flat-out run away. But her bolting days were over. Tenley glanced at Jade in the rearview mirror. She loved taking care of Jade even if the circumstances that had led them to this point were anything but ideal. You couldn't help but love the girl, and love her Tenley did.

Seeing Mac at church had started something she didn't know how to stop. Their past planted a wall between them. A wall built of her indiscretions and her refusal to fully reveal herself to the man she'd loved.

Relegating Mac to her past took more effort than she'd anticipated. In typical Mac fashion, he blew up any opposition that dared stand in his way. He was a trailblazer on a mission to take on his responsibility. He loved Jade,

Tenley knew that as well as she knew her own name. But did he see Jade, truly see her, in the way that she needed? That question kept Tenley awake at night and dug her heels in when it came to Mac ripping Jade away from this place and the people who knew and loved her.

They reached Tenley's house and Jade leaped out. "I'm going to get my boots and hat." She raced into the house, Tenley following behind at a slower pace.

Mac's truck rumbled up behind hers. He killed the engine and stepped out, still wearing his jeans and pressed blue shirt from church. He reached into the truck and retrieved the black ball cap he'd worn every day since he walked back into her life.

"Give us five minutes." Tenley called over her shoulder while following Jade. She closed the door behind her, an obvious dismissal and refusal to allow him into her house. Her mother would be ashamed, but Tenley had precious few moments to preserve her sanity from Mac, and if rudeness was what it took, then, she'd close a hundred doors in his face.

Jade ran back out of the room where she'd been sleeping these last months, her new tan Stetson clutched to her chest and her boots peeking from her too-long jeans. "Can I show Uncle Mac around the barn?"

"Wait for me." Tenley held up a hand to stop the argument brewing. "You can sit on the porch, but do not go to the barn without me."

"Okay." Jade groused, but her bad mood didn't last long once she whipped the front door open and spotted Mac sitting in one of Tenley's rocking chairs.

Tenley made quick work of changing from her pink, flowy skirt to her favorite pair of jeans. She carried her boots outside and sat on the top step to yank them on.

Mac and Jade stood in the middle of the porch, waiting with matching frowns.

"You two keep making that face and one day it's going to get stuck like that." Tenley stood and grinned as her mom's words came out. Once upon a time, she'd believed it and had spent hours trying to make her face stick in one expression. Those lessons had come in handy later when she needed a mask to wear when she was deep in her alcoholism.

Jade cocked her head to the side. "Really?" She eyed Mac, tiptoeing to see his face. "Wow, Uncle Mac. Yours must already be stuck."

Mac startled. The frown deepened, a groove appearing between his eyebrows.

Tenley reached out and smoothed her thumb over the deepening line. Her breath stuttered at the look Mac shot her way. Equal parts shock and memory. "Smile, Mac." She forced her own lips to move. "Like this. See? Easy."

Mac grinned back in a knowing sort of way. Maybe the damage wasn't completely done, and besides, he looked rather adorable with the wrinkles of additional years.

Jade clapped and then grabbed his hand. "Let's go."

Thankfully, all thoughts of how well Mac had aged fled under Jade's enthusiasm. Tenley chuckled and followed the pair. Jade skipped alongside Mac's long strides and talked a mile a minute all the way to the barn.

Luke shot out from his and Molly's house, one hand holding his hat on his head and the other waving frantically. "Wait for me."

Molly hurried out onto the porch.

"I got him." She joined Molly, the steps creaking when she jumped up.

Molly put a hand to her throat. A flicker of unease raced across her face. "You sure you don't mind?"

"Luke is always welcome to ride with us." Tenley gripped her sister's arm in a quick squeeze. "We'll be back in a few hours."

Molly nodded but didn't return to the house.

Tenley jogged to catch up with Mac and the kids at the barn door. Both Jade and Luke stopped at the line where light met shadow. Their toes brushed the dark interior of the barn, but they didn't move inside.

Mac lifted his eyebrows and glanced at Tenley. "Thought we were riding."

"They know they're not allowed inside the barn unless they're with me or Brody." Tenley smiled at the upturned faces. "Good job, guys. Thanks for following the rules. It would've been easy to assume that you were allowed to go in with Mac since he's an adult, but thank you for waiting."

They shot matching smiles at her, the looks tugging at her heart. They could be brother and sister standing there.

Mac huffed a sound that might've been appreciation but sounded an awful lot like annoyance.

Tenley stepped into the barn, the kids on her heels. "Mac, do you need help with your horse? How long has it been since you rode?"

"I'm fine." One side of his mouth quirked up in a semblance of a smile. At least he was trying. Clearing his throat, Mac rubbed a hand over his forehead. The cap shifted on his dark hair before he tugged it back in place. "I haven't forgotten how to ride. Just point me at which horse I can use."

Tenley paused on her trek down the barn aisle. Horses greeted them from both sides, several stretching their noses toward Tenley in hopes of getting a treat or a pat. "Jade, you can take Snowflake today."

"And I'm riding Ranger." Luke stood in front of his horse's stall. He held out his hand and Ranger—the black-and-white paint that Brody found for Luke's last birthday—nudged Luke's palm.

"Right. You can bring your horses out and start brushing them."

"Is that a good idea? Letting them take care of their horses by themselves?" The pleasant wrinkles in his face deepened, carving trenches between his eyes. But it wasn't anger or frustration. Was he afraid?

Tenley grabbed his sleeve and pulled him farther away from the kids. "They're safe with their horses, Mac. I've been riding with these kids since they could climb on a horse. I've taught them well and I'd never put them in a bad spot."

He flinched away at her touch but sighed, sounding resigned. "You and I both know that horses can be unpredictable. It's been years. I don't know who you are anymore. Maybe not even back then." The sadness coming off his voice pulled at her heart.

"Six years, eleven months, ten days, five hours." Tenley rattled off the exact numbers since she'd broken Mac's heart. The hours since she'd hit rock bottom and knew that she had to let Mac go…for both of their sakes. The months since she'd checked into rehab and sobered up. "But who's counting, right?" She gave a careless shrug and pivoted on her heel. "You can ride the black mare." Tenley pointed at the stall. "Her name's Midnight."

"You keep track?" His question burrowed deep and offered a quiet reprieve.

"Of the worst moment of my life?" She kept her back to

him, afraid of what she'd see if she turned around. "Yeah, Mac. I keep track."

"You're not what I expected." The sound of his footsteps told her Mac had moved to the stall door.

Tenley gave herself a moment to collect her thoughts and turned. "Mac?"

He tensed, his body turning rigid.

She continued before she lost her nerve. "I'm not asking for you to forgive me, but can we at least put aside the animosity long enough for the kids to enjoy this ride? I don't want to be your enemy. I never wanted that."

"What did you want?" Mac ran his hand over the mare's coal-black face and his eyes softened when he caught Tenley watching him. "You left me, Ten. You shut me out and I still don't know why."

The sound of the nickname he'd given her in middle school gutted her. While everyone else labeled her troublesome, Mac called her Ten as a way of easing the hurt. Brody and Molly picked up on it later and it had carried over even after Mac took off for Chicago.

The answer to his unasked question perched on the tip of her tongue, the facts that would push him away for good. A boulder lodged in her throat, and she took a step back. "Because you were too good for me. I'd made too many mistakes, Mac. Mistakes that I've finally forgiven myself for and put behind me."

He shoved the cap back and ran a hand across his head. "What does that mean?"

"I—"

"Can we saddle the horses now?" Luke's voice carried down the barn aisle.

Tenley spun away from Mac, her heart hammering like

she'd been caught with her hand in her mama's cookie jar. "Sure. I'll help you."

She spent the next several minutes helping Jade and Luke put their saddles in place while her heartbeat slowed toward normal. She tightened cinches and double-checked the bridles were on properly. All as a means of avoiding Mac and the conversation she knew they needed to have. Was it selfishness or self-preservation that had her unwilling to reveal the facts of that night, to wait and postpone watching the last of the light dim from his eyes when he discovered what she'd done?

Mac led his horse from the barn behind Luke and Jade. He paused beside Tenley and threaded the reins through his hands. "I'll watch them while you get your horse."

"Thanks." Unlike Mac, she had no qualms about putting the kids' safety in his hands. She tried not to rush through brushing and saddling Romeo, the bay gelding she usually rode on these trail rides. She led him from the barn and blinked to clear the sudden glare of sunlight from her eyes as she settled her Stetson on her head.

Mac stood with his back to her. Jade and Luke sat on the fence railing in front of him, seemingly mesmerized by whatever Mac was saying. Tenley crept forward on silent feet until she stood close enough to knock the cap from Mac's head. She did so with enough enthusiasm to send the hat spinning through the air.

She didn't know what had come over her.

Mac whirled around, eyes blazing.

Tenley's laugh rang out. She held up the battered brown cowboy hat she'd hidden behind her back. "You're not going out with us without the proper attire." She gripped the hat's brim and stood on her tiptoes to slide the Stetson onto Mac's head.

His gaze locked on to her face. As quickly as the tension gathered, it released in a shared breath.

Her fingertips grazed his ears. The pulse in his neck jumped, and her heart joined its beat. She jerked back and nearly stumbled into her horse.

"My old hat." Mac's voice was throaty and deep.

Did the memories flow through him as easily as they did her?

"I found it in the office." She lifted one shoulder. "Thought you might want it back." She remembered the day he'd left it there. The day after the wedding debacle. He'd come here demanding answers, and she'd denied him that then, the same as she did now. She'd watched from her room, pausing from packing her bag for rehab, to see him stomp into the barn. He came out minutes later, appearing disgusted and hatless.

Brody had never told her what transpired during those few minutes. She hadn't been strong enough back then, or in the years since, to ask.

Putting her foot in the stirrup, she swung into the saddle.

Luke and Jade jumped from the fence and led their horses over to the mounting block.

Mac stood back, watching. He waited until they were both safe in the saddle and standing alongside Tenley to swing into his. He gathered up the reins. "Where should we ride to?"

"The ridge." Luke stood in his stirrups and pointed at the small path leading deep into the woods. It started near Brody's house, the line of oaks, maples and hickories causing the trail to disappear unless you knew where to look.

"Yeah," Jade agreed with a whoop.

Tenley eyed Mac, noting the way his jaw tightened.

He didn't argue, merely dipped his head in a nod. "Let's go, then."

His tone was less than enthusiastic. Tenley let it go. She no longer had the right to call Mac out on his moods. She could ask all the questions she wanted. He didn't owe her any answers. Not after the way she'd ended things.

Luke and Jade rode side by side, chattering like magpies.

Tenley envied the ease between them. "Is it too much to ask for us to be friends?"

"I think it's best if we aren't." He settled into the mare's stride with the years of muscle memory taking hold, though he held the reins with a stiffness she didn't remember.

"We share guardianship, Mac. Jade deserves for us to at least try not to shoot daggers at each other every time we're in each other's sight." She tried to keep the desperation from her voice but failed.

"We share it *for now*," Mac said meaningfully. He patted his mare's neck and glanced over at her. The heat of his gaze tore away the layers created by years of distance and left her cut to the bone. "I'm only staying until the end of the school year. Once I talk to Leonard and get this mess sorted out, Jade comes back to Chicago with me. I'm her blood. You and I know the court's going to rule in my favor. It's the only way to resolve this—" his left hand pawed the air "—whatever *this* is."

Mac moved away, his body taut and eyes holding a smolder of something she didn't recognize. The loss pained her, all the way to her bones. What happened to put the look of doom in the depths of his eyes? She opened her mouth to ask, but it was written in every conversation they'd had recently. Mac had lost everyone he loved. If she didn't know better, she'd think he felt guilty.

Tenley locked the words away in a vault. Mac's past belonged to him. If she tried to find her way in, she risked losing herself to his charm.

They stepped into the shade of the overarching trees. A shudder rippled down Tenley's spine that had nothing to do with the sudden change in light and temperature and everything to do with the man riding at her side. She was going to lose Jade.

After everything she'd done to him, Mac had found a way to exact his revenge.

Mac regretted his harshness, if not the words themselves. Tenley poked at him, prodding his old wounds, tearing them open, exposing them to the light of a new day. He couldn't start over with her, not now and not ever.

Tenley rode alongside him. She faced forward, her spine arrow straight and her gaze on Jade and Luke. The kids never stopped talking, a fact Mac was thankful for. They didn't need to hear any of his and Tenley's troubles.

Oak leaves dotted the ground, their purled edges showing streaks of brown and gold, left over from the previous autumn. No trace of stress marred Tenley's face. She sat relaxed in the saddle, wrists crossed over the saddle horn. She dipped her chin toward him. "Been a while."

For so many things. He relaxed into the horse's stride. "I missed this in Chicago."

"What? You mean you didn't demand a spot on the mounted police force?" Her nose crinkled. "That's a thing, right?" A laugh bubbled out of her, edged with sadness she couldn't hide from him.

"Yeah." His laugh joined hers before an avalanche of grief cut him off. "I wanted to be known as more than the country cop."

Hooves struck dirt, the steady thud-thud excavating the pain. Mac pushed hair from his forehead, tucking it under the hat brim, and breathed in the smell of horse and leather. They fell into old habits too easily. Confronting each other one minute and able to laugh the next.

"Did you make it?"

"Make what?" He'd lost the conversation, distracted by Tenley's quiet presence and the swish of horses' tails.

She sent a glance his way. Thoughtful in her perusal. "Were you more than a country cop in the big city?"

"Yeah." And look what came of it.

"What was Chicago like?" She ducked under a low-hanging branch. It snagged her hair, pulling the pony-tail taut.

Mac reached over and freed her but didn't let himself revel in the moment. In the softness of her hair and the fact that she didn't pull away from him. Spinning the green-and-brown twig by its stem, he focused on the colors whirling. He contemplated his response.

"I loved the constant action. They put me with an older officer, let him show me the ropes." He tossed the stick aside. "I married Laura. Lost her. Then nearly lost my partner. Lost Amber. Came back here to get Jade."

The years between his leaving and recent return condensed into a monotone announcement that held none of the anger and shame. His life was not a storybook for Tenley to read late at night.

Tenley's face registered shock. "I'm sorry." Tenley threaded her fingers through her mount's mane and turned her face away from him. "Amber told me about Laura."

A peculiar note in her voice tugged at him. Jealousy? Anger? Neither made sense. Tenley hadn't wanted him.

He deserved to find happiness wherever he could, and Laura had made him happy.

"Don't you think Jade deserves the chance to have us both in her life?" Tenley's question was soft. "She's lost her parents. I know you're probably right—" she choked over the words "—about the court. But please don't take her away from everything that she knows."

Mac tightened his grip on the reins, then relaxed it before his tension traveled through to the horse and made her anxious.

"Maybe that's exactly what she needs. A fresh start in a new place."

Tenley scoffed. "Like you." She scrubbed a hand over her face. "Sorry. That was rude."

"I'm not the one who quit, Tenley. You did." He nudged his horse closer, until their knees almost brushed. "You left me first, and I couldn't stay in this town another minute knowing that I might run into you and have to see that dead look in your eyes that said you'd stopped loving me."

"I never…" She trailed off and lifted her head to the sky. Sunlight caught the curve of her chin and deepened the lashes fanning out across her cheeks. She rode with her eyes closed, trusting her horse in a way that was pure Tenley. It ripped away the last of the bandages covering his scabbed heart and exposed him to the light.

Mac's pulse skipped. "What?" He ground his teeth together. The need to hear her answer shouldn't hook straight into his heart and draw him around. But it did. After all this time, after all he'd done to put her aside, it always came back to Tenley.

A grunt of dismissal left him. He'd loved Laura. He'd fought the cancer alongside her, every step of the way.

When she wasn't strong enough to fight on her own, he put in enough to carry them both through.

Still, one look at Tenley and he felt like a teenager all over again. She twisted him up inside unlike anyone else.

"You never what?" He forced out the question, desperate for an answer that might alleviate the pounding in his head and the constant drive for peace when he thought of her.

She met his gaze head on. "I never stopped." She shook her head, a sad look entering her eyes. "What I did, I did for your own good."

"Funny how I can't believe that." He reined his horse sideways, putting space between them. Her response fueled more questions. "I never wanted to come back here." He rolled the stiffness from his shoulder.

"So why did you?"

"Jade." His niece's name rolled from him like thunder through the sky. "She's all I have now, and I'll protect her with everything I have."

"Even from me." Tenley looked at him, then ahead where Jade rode. "I'm not some monster you need to protect her from. I love her like she's my own. I've been here the whole time, part of her life since she took her first breath."

Mac fought to keep himself in check. It did neither of them any good to keep rehashing these same topics. He locked his jaw tight. "I'm going to ride with Jade." He urged his mount into a trot and caught up with Jade's white pony. Schooling his expression, he grinned at her. "Hey, kiddo."

Jade beamed at Mac, bouncing in her saddle. "Wait till you see the ridge. It's so pretty. Tenley says it's her favorite trail."

"Is that so?" Mac resisted the urge to look at Tenley. They used to ride this trail together all the time. He'd proposed at the top of the ridge that overlooked Tamarack Springs. Would Tenley take him back there after the harsh words they'd spoken?

Luke leaned forward and patted his horse's neck. "Uncle Brody says it's a good spot for finding God." He wrinkled his nose. "I keep looking, but I haven't seen Him yet. You think we might see Him today?"

The simplicity of Luke's question battered Mac's heart. He'd gone to church for as long as he could remember. He'd trusted God with every piece of himself, until it seemed God didn't want him anymore. His heart had been crushed and torn apart. Laura sewed the pieces back together and he'd thought maybe God was there then. Until it all came apart at the seams. Everyone he'd ever loved, God took away.

Mac swallowed hard as he rode alongside Jade. Tenley appeared in his peripheral. *God, please. Don't take them too.* Them. He tugged his hat lower over his forehead and breathed in slow and steady breaths until his heart settled back into a normal rhythm. He didn't love Tenley. They were past all that.

Weren't they?

"I think you can find God no matter where you are." Tenley spoke up from behind Mac. She reassured Luke when Mac couldn't. "Some places make it easier to open up and see Him, but all it takes is a willing heart."

Luke continued patting Ranger's neck.

They rode with nothing but birdsong and the horses' thudding hooves as background noise. Each of them lost in their own thoughts. The ridge appeared, slowly at first.

A hint of open sky through the trees. Greens of every variety mingling together and swaying in the breeze.

Mac emerged first, followed by Jade and Luke. They lined up at the edge of the path, facing the deep valley. Tamarack Springs appeared in flits of color that dotted the landscape. The red roof from the Langleys' Bed and Breakfast where he'd been staying. Tan and white from the library sitting in a little corner away from the main center of town, which was concentrated on diners and shops. And Leonard's office.

Mac rested his wrists on the saddle horn and let the mare lower her head to sniff the ground. Tomorrow, he'd learn what his options were. Whether he had a chance of cutting Tenley out of Jade's life. It hurt him to consider how Jade might react to that. Later. He'd deal with that later.

Tenley leaned over and whispered to Luke, her voice too low for Mac to hear.

Luke nodded at whatever Tenley said and wiped his eyes.

Jade scooted sideways and patted Luke's back. Their easy friendship reminded Mac of him and Tenley. They'd always known when the other needed comfort or when they needed space to work things out by themselves.

Until they didn't. Until Tenley walked away without a backward glance.

She shot a look at him like she felt his gaze on her now, and he snapped his head around to the view. His mare snorted and lifted her head. Mac tightened his grip on the reins and eyed the terrain. "You should have a fence up here. It's dangerous to let riders be able to get this close to the edge."

"I'll let Brody know you don't approve." Tenley's spoke

sharply, her tone cutting. She reined her horse around. "We should head back."

Surprisingly, the kids didn't argue but spent most of their time looking from Tenley at the front of their little parade to Mac taking up the rear.

Jade looked at Luke and shrugged.

"Aunt Tenley, can we race back?" Luke asked with a sideways glance at Jade.

"Oh yeah. Let's go." Jade urged her pony faster.

Mac rode closer to Jade. "Hold up. You can't go faster than a trot on these trails."

"He's right. You both know the rules." Tenley agreed with what sounded like begrudging respect. She caught his gaze and lifted an eyebrow in a clear challenge. "What about it, Mac? The trail from the trees to the barn was always our racetrack. Care to see if you can beat me?"

She was goading him. No surprise, really.

"Please, Uncle Mac?" Jade folded her hands under her chin. "Pretty please? We'll be careful."

Sure. Galloping at full speed was being careful. Past races with Tenley nudged at him. He remembered the first time he'd raced her down that trail. They'd barely been Jade's age, and her dad had laughed as he ran alongside them on his own horse. Mac closed his eyes, attempting to hold on to the joy he'd felt then instead of the aching emptiness he endured.

His eyes snapped open. "Let's do it."

A trio of whoops filled the air. Tenley's smile was the stuff songs were written about. It filled her face with such absolute joy that it took his breath.

She reined around and waited for him. "Luke, you and Jade go first. Mac and I will be behind you. Ride toward the round pen. Once you pass the last fence, slow your horse."

"I know." Jade bounced in her saddle. "Let's go, Luke."

"On three." Tenley held her gelding back, coming alongside Mac. "One. Two. Three."

On three, both ponies launched forward. Laughter rang out, the kids' giggles floating on the wind. Ranger and Snowflake raced along, nose to nose.

Mac gave himself permission to enjoy the moment instead of worrying over the what-ifs. Jade and Luke sped past the last fence, then slowed their mounts.

Tenley glanced at him. "Ready?"

Not in the least. He nodded anyway.

"Let's see what you remember, cowboy." Tenley tapped the brim of his hat and laughed when he scowled. "Just like old times."

That's what he was afraid of. She counted them down and bolted on three, with Mac reacting a half second later. They thundered down the dirt path, his bones jarring with every stride. The mare smoothed out, stretching her neck and straining forward.

Tenley sped alongside him, her hands deep in her mount's mane. They pulled ahead, and Tenley shot him a smile of victory.

"Oh no you don't." Mac urged the mare faster, bringing her back in line with Tenley's gelding. The mare crept ahead by a nose, then a head. By the time they flashed past the fence, Tenley's gelding's nose was behind Mac's stirrup, making him the undisputed winner. He reined back to a trot, then a walk.

Tenley thwacked his hat again, knocking it down over his eyes.

Clapping sounded from Mac's left. He propped the hat

up and scoured the area to find Margaret, Peter, Brody, Molly and a woman he vaguely recognized standing in the shade under the barn's sloping roof.

Mac stopped the mare and dismounted.

Brody approached, a sly grin showing as he slapped Mac between the shoulder blades. "About time you won a race against Tenley."

"Just wait until I get Shadow running." Tenley groused from the side. She dismounted and patted her gelding's neck. "No offense, Romeo."

"Shadow?" Mac returned Brody's back-slapping hug. They'd been friends long before Mac and Tenley became a thing, and Brody was another person Mac had left behind for a life in Chicago. It seemed only fair. Brody was Tenley's brother. Of course he had her back when Mac's world came crashing down.

Brody answered for Tenley. "Tenley rescued Shadow from the auction last month. Been trying to train her, but she's not having any part of it."

Tenley led her gelding into the barn. "I'll get through to her. She just needs time to learn to trust me."

Molly helped Luke with his horse, while the familiar woman helped Jade.

Brody stepped forward. "Mac, you might remember Callie. She spent summers with us as kids."

"And now she stays with us all the time." Tenley added. "They got married a few months ago."

"Wait." Mac shook his head to clear it. "Callie." He snapped his fingers. "I remember. You left to ride in the rodeo. Barrel racing, right?"

"Yep." She pulled Snowflake's saddle free and headed toward the tack room. "Came back when my horse went blind. Brody helped me retrain her." And they'd picked up where they left off? There was more to this story than he was being told. But he remembered the devastation that rocked Brody all those years ago when his dad was in the accident that paralyzed him and Callie left after Brody proposed.

Whoa. Mac scuffed a hand over his cheek.

Talk about small-town life.

Talk about forgiveness.

Callie was back. Mac was back.

But not for good, he reminded himself. *No, sir.*

Few more weeks and he'd return where he belonged.

Chapter Six

Mac left Leonard's office on Monday morning with enough weight on his shoulders to send him to the ground. He fought to straighten his bones and shore up his muscles to bear the responsibility anchoring him to Tamarack Springs. Sheriff Hanks was right. Amber had left her house—and her daughter—to Mac. He refused to allow Tenley to keep her temporary position in Jade's life. He was being harsh, but it was for Jade's own good.

He slid into his truck and leaned his forehead on the steering wheel. "What were you thinking, Amber?" He understood giving him guardianship of Jade. Giving it to Tenley too was what kept coming back to him. Amber couldn't have known that this would happen to her and her husband. No one could've known. It was a worst-case scenario. How often had he seen that play out during his years in Chicago? Too many. Thank goodness Amber and her husband had a will. Otherwise, Jade might've ended up in foster care until he recuperated enough to bring her home.

He wasn't ready for what lay at the end of Amber's paved drive. For the house he'd need to empty and sell before returning to Chicago. He pinched the bridge of his nose. This meant he could leave his room at the B and B and move into Amber's house in the meantime. Zeus would appreciate the fenced-in backyard.

What about Jade? The question pummeled him into cranking the truck and heading toward Amber's. He'd do what he could with the house until he could talk to her. Which meant seeing Tenley again.

She'd showed up in his dreams last night. Flashes of memories, times long past when one look from her sent Mac's heart into overdrive. He'd loved her so deeply that losing her was like losing half of himself. Their ride together had stirred him into remembering better times. Times that he ought to leave well enough alone.

Hours later, he rolled up to Tenley's house amid a flurry of activity. Molly and Luke hurried past. Luke waved at him. "Where's Zeus?"

"Resting." He'd left Zeus in his crate for an afternoon nap. The dog was sleeping more lately. Mac chose to take it as a sign of Zeus's healing.

Mac stepped out of his truck and popped the hat Tenley had returned to him onto his head. It fit as snug as ever, yet another reminder of times gone by. "What's going on?" He shot the question at Brody when the man rushed from the barn.

Brody spun on his heel. "Hey, man. Been trying to call you since yesterday. We decided to have an impromptu anniversary dinner for Mom and Dad tonight. They wanted you to come."

"Me?" He palmed the back of his neck.

"Doesn't matter how long you've been gone. You're still part of the family as far as they're concerned." Brody waved in a hurry-up motion. "Come on. They'll be excited you made it."

"I need to talk to Jade." Mac picked up the pace until he was jogging alongside Brody.

"She'll be at the house. Saw her and Tenley headed that way a bit ago. Probably decorating or something. You know how Tenley loves to spruce these parties up."

A memory came unbidden. The night before the wedding. He'd been exhausted, nervous, excited. And Tenley. Man, Tenley just kept going. She fussed with every flower and shifted every tablecloth. He'd tried to get her to leave it alone and go home to rest. She'd ushered him out of the reception hall with assurances that she was almost done.

He'd offered to stay, but she said it was something she wanted to do herself. He remembered watching her from the doorway for a few minutes. Noted the dark shadows around her eyes and how she leaned on the tables like she needed their support. She'd dragged a hand down her face and bowed her head. And instead of going in to ask what was wrong, he'd left, assuming the nerves he felt were the only problem between them.

How wrong he'd been.

Mac followed Brody down the rutted drive and nearly pitched straight into Brody's back when his boot landed in a hole. He staggered upright and nudged his hat from his eyes. "You ever regret staying?" He didn't know why he asked, or what answer he expected.

Brody leaped over the porch steps and pulled open the screen door. He spared a glance at Mac before heading inside. "Used to, sure. But not now. I'm right where I'm supposed to be."

Callie met Brody in the middle of the living room and embraced him.

A pang of jealousy shot through Mac before he could control it. Jade skipped into the room, ribbons trailing behind her. She held up the spool of bright red. "Help, Uncle Mac. I can't reach to put this on the door."

He swept Jade into his arms and lifted her to his shoulder. "Your wish is my command."

Her giggle drove away the lingering sadness. They worked together to drape the ribbon over the arched entryway separating the living room and dining room. The cozy space where he'd crashed after football games and weekends wrapped around him. Everything looked the same, from the hardwood floors to the tattered brown sofa.

Margaret, Molly, Tenley and Callie moved around the kitchen. Molly slid a cake onto the counter at the same time Brody bumped into Tenley, who took a step back and knocked her elbow into Molly's side.

Mac lunged, lowering Jade and throwing out a hand to stop the cake from sliding off the counter. His palm hit the cardboard under the cake and his fingers slid into the icing. The cake wobbled but remained on the counter.

"Nice save." Brody clapped Mac's shoulder. "Just like the old days on the football field, huh?"

"Glad I didn't try to tuck it under my arm and run to the end zone." Mac snorted and reached for the towel Tenley extended to him without saying a word.

He eyed the cake, where he'd left a hand-shaped imprint behind. "Sorry, Molly."

She waved a hand. "No biggie. I can fix that. It hitting the floor would've been a different story."

"Just call me saving-the-day Mac." He laughed while wiping icing from his hand.

A look crossed Tenley's face. One that begged a million questions. None of which he could ask here in front of everyone. She pursed her lips and turned away before Mac could do something foolish like reach for her.

The bottom layer of Molly's cake was a square, while the layer atop that was a circle. White icing swirled with hints of blue and gold spun around the perimeter of both layers. A banner hung across the top, with Peter and Margaret's names written out in cursive letters that twined together so that he couldn't tell where one ended and the next began. Molly had always had a gift, but this was next level. Maybe some things had changed?

The Jacobs family piled into the dining room. Before Mac realized what happened, the only chair left was next to Tenley. She eyed him, the look almost challenging, daring him to ask for a different seat.

Not happening.

He firmed his resolve to keep his emotional distance and accepted the seat. Jade sat on the other side of Tenley, and he stretched an arm behind Tenley to tweak Jade's ponytail.

She squealed and smacked at his hand.

Peter bowed his head, a prayer ready.

Mac ducked his own head, realizing then that he'd invaded this dinner with his presence. He didn't belong here anymore. Before he could stand and get away, Peter's low timbre drew him into the peace and comfort the Jacobs always gave him.

It wrapped around him, as real and tangible as an embrace, pinning him to his seat.

Mac rolled his shoulders, attempting to rid himself of the feeling. He didn't deserve it, and he couldn't let himself fall into the trap of thinking that anyone wanted him here.

Tenley's hands clenched in her lap.

Mac watched her through lidded eyes as she twisted the napkin between her hands, wringing it into a knotted mess. He gripped her wrist, having moved without thought to offer comfort.

Tenley's hand spasmed under his, and her head jerked in his direction.

Mac squeezed again, then released.

Heads lifted around the table, and in typical Jacobs' fashion, chaos ensued. Conversations swirled around Mac, many of which he didn't understand. Jade chatted with Luke across the table, and Tenley focused on her plate like it was the most interesting thing in the world.

Mac let everything roll over him, doing everything he could to keep his heart from engaging.

Once the meal finished, Mac followed Jade and Tenley out onto the porch.

Jade climbed into the porch swing. Tenley put it into motion with a gentle push before sitting down in one of the rocking chairs that matched the pair on her own front porch.

"Tenley, I need to talk to Jade." Mac tucked his thumbs into his belt and gave the front door a pointed look. "Alone."

"No." She shook her head. "Anything you need to say can be said in front of me."

"You don't trust me with my own niece?" Indignation drove his voice into a growl.

Tenley crossed her arms. Her chin jutted forward in that stubborn tilt he knew achingly well. She'd made up her mind and nothing would change it now. It reminded him of Brody and years of arguments between the siblings. Arguments he'd mediated to the best of his ability, even when they involved his best friend and his girlfriend. Never a good place to be, by his reckoning.

Mac scrubbed a hand over his head and stopped the swing long enough to settle in beside Jade. She scooted next to him, tucking herself into his side and looking up at him with gem-green eyes. "What's wrong, Uncle Mac?"

"Nothing." He fought back a rush of grief. "I stopped by your house today." He waited to see how she'd react. He needed to know her feelings before he proceeded.

Jade dropped her gaze to her lap and twisted the hem of her shirt around her thumb. It hit him with a jolt, how often he'd seen Tenley do the same thing when she was nervous.

He shot a look at Tenley and found her watching them with inscrutable eyes.

"I miss home," Jade admitted in a whisper.

Mac's breath rushed out. "Well, that's what I wanted to talk to you about. Your mom and dad gave me the house." He cleared his throat of a boulder when Jade whipped a look at him so full of hope and love that it near to choked him. "I'm thinking about staying there, if that's okay with you?"

She nodded, her chin quivering.

Mac ignored the deep gasp from Tenley and plunged ahead. "And you can stay with me. If you want to."

Jade swiveled from his face to Tenley's and back. "What about Tenley? And the horses? Can I bring Rascal?"

"We'll work something out." Mac made the promise with all the assurance he could dredge up. He'd work everything out. That was his job now, to protect Jade. She was all he had left.

"Jade, I think Molly's about to cut the cake. Why don't

you grab a piece and eat with Luke." Tenley stood and held open the screen door.

Jade slid from the swing, Mac forgotten in the anticipation of sugary sweets.

Tenley closed the door behind Jade and faced Mac with her arms crossed. The only word that came to mind when he looked at her was *furious*. She was absolutely furious with him.

He couldn't say that he blamed her. "She belongs with me."

"She's not a possession you can cart around from place to place. She needs stability." Tenley crossed to the swing and poked a finger at him. "You didn't tell her about Chicago. You made it sound like she'll be staying home forever. You have to tell her the truth, Mac."

"And what's the truth, Tenley?" He stood, peering down at her. "The truth is that I'm never going to stay here. Tamarack Springs isn't home anymore. I'm moving back to Chicago as soon as school's over. I thought you'd accepted that." Not true. He'd known she would fight. He recognized the instincts kicking up in Tenley from the minute he walked back onto the ranch. He pinched the bridge of his nose and rolled the stiffness from his shoulder. "Let's not make this any harder than it has to be."

"I'm not the one who's using a child as leverage for revenge." She sniffed and tears sheened her eyes. "Don't do this, Mac. Please. Don't take her away." There was more to the plea than the simple words spoken between them.

"You asked what happened to me." Mac didn't know why he pushed now, when they were so close to touching that he felt her breath rush across his cheek. He needed to see her reaction. He needed to understand her the way they used to be, before she gave him the heave-ho without a thought.

Tenley's gaze roamed his face, then tracked to his shoulder that he gripped tight to still the aching.

"I lost my parents, you, Laura and then Amber." Saying it out loud wrenched his heart like it was the first time. "I can't lose Jade too. I won't lose someone else that I love." He tightened his grip on his shoulder and straightened. "I'll stay until school's over, then we're leaving. I've already talked to Leonard about sole custody. He's going to talk to the judge."

Tenley backed away from him, her hand clasped tight around her throat. "You can't..." She trailed off and then shook her head, weaving side to side in slow motion. "I'm sorry, Mac. I'm sorry I never explained why I couldn't marry you."

"It doesn't matter." He slashed a hand through the air. "It's in the past. Let's just move on. Jade is the only thing I care about now."

Tenley tensed but didn't speak. The heartbreak in her eyes ripped through him. She spun on her heel and raced down the drive. She left him standing there alone, and though she no longer loved him, the feeling of abandonment tightened his gut.

Mac watched her go until she disappeared into the barn. Was he making a mistake? His heart twisted, begging him to reconsider the decisions he'd made since coming home. No. This was no longer home. It would never be home.

He didn't belong in this place of peace. Scrubbing his palms over his eyes, he opened the door and stepped back inside. He'd let Tenley get to him yesterday during the trail ride. She'd given him a glimpse of what they could have been, and his heart couldn't take the beating of loving her again just to have her toss him aside. Better for him and everyone else if he guarded himself against her and the feelings he'd spent years learning how to cage.

Tenley heaved. Her stomach roiled against Mac's angry words. She'd had a chance to tell him the truth, about her, about the past and the wedding, and she'd chickened out. Because once he knew, he'd pack up Jade and leave. He wouldn't wait another day, much less another week and a half while Jade finished school.

She pushed tears from her eyes and opened Shadow's stall. The mare backed away and tucked her body into the corner farthest away from Tenley. Crooning, Tenley latched the door behind her and squeezed her eyes shut.

"God, I've made a mess of it all." She slid down the wall and drew her knees to her chest. Her sobs mingled with her muffled words, creating a cry only God could understand. She had to fix this. Somehow. "I can't do this alone." She gripped her calves and lifted her head, banging it on the wooden wall.

The mare shuffled her hooves and snorted a low breath in Tenley's direction.

"Sorry, Shadow." Tenley stayed curled into herself while the mare adjusted to her presence. She'd made great strides this week in training Shadow. The mare still didn't quite trust her, but they were getting close.

Tenley picked up a handful of hay, shredding it into tiny bits. "I've changed too, you know. I used to hurt everyone who got too close. I knew that I'd do the same thing to Mac. So I pushed him away in the only way that I knew he'd never forgive." What a mistake. If she was a stronger person, she would've told him everything years ago.

Now it was too late. There was no moving forward for them.

Footsteps sounded down the aisle. Tenley's heart leaped in hopes that Mac had come after her.

Instead, she heard Brody's voice calling her name.

"In here." Tenley stuck her fingers over the stall door and wiggled them. She could've ignored him, but, like her, Brody was too stubborn for his own good. He wouldn't leave the barn until he tracked her down.

"Right where I thought you'd be." He draped both bronzed forearms over the door and tipped his head at her.

Tenley avoided his gaze. "Here to tell me you were right? That I should've left well enough alone?"

Brody opened the stall door and nudged her with his booted toe. "Scoot over."

She did as he ordered, sliding through the shavings until he had enough room to close the door and sit. He grunted while stretching out his long legs. "I know I've not been the best brother over the years. But I'd like to think that I wouldn't rub your nose in your mistakes."

Tenley harrumphed. The mare startled at the sound, and Tenley made gentle shushing sounds until Shadow settled. "Until Callie came back, you delighted in trying to manage me and my life. Along with everyone else. You took on the responsibility of the whole ranch, Dad's medical bills. Everything. And heaven forbid anyone try to help."

Brody removed his hat and slid a hand through his hair. He nodded, a muscle feathering his jaw. "You're right. I did all that. Until I couldn't anymore. It nearly broke me, Ten. I don't want that for you."

"I can't let Mac take Jade away." She tightened her grip on her legs, digging her fingers into her calves until they ached. "He's going to try and contest the will. Take my guardianship away."

Brody whistled through his teeth. "Then we'll fight. Together." He squeezed her shoulder. "You don't have to do everything alone either. Mom, Dad and Molly will all stand with us on this. Jade is part of the family too." He gave her a long look from the side. "We both got extra doses of stubbornness. I personally blame Dad."

Tenley managed to grin at the running Jacobs' family joke.

"I made a promise to you years ago, that I'd stand by your side. I'm here. Whatever you need." He gripped her shoulder and pulled her into a side hug.

"You never agreed with my decision to cut Mac loose." Tenley muttered into his shoulder.

Brody's arm tightened across her shoulders. "I wanted you to tell him the truth. About the alcoholism. About rehab. I still think he deserves to know, but that's your choice."

"It ruined your friendship with him. I ruined everything."

"Stop." Brody leaned far enough away to meet her gaze. When she tried to look away, he ducked his head, forcing her to see him. "You're forgiven. For all of that. Don't let yourself get trapped in that spiral of regret. You did what you had to do to get better. You're stronger than you know. Stronger than I am."

Strength. What did that mean exactly? She didn't feel strong. She felt weak and helpless. And like a failure.

But Brody had a point. She'd pushed back against her alcoholism, and with God's help, she'd won. Almost seven years sober. A fact she never wanted to take for granted.

"Callie's been good for you." Tenley poked Brody in the shoulder.

Brody's laughter rang out, loud and long. "No kidding. Wasn't a picnic reaching this point though. We both know that anything worth having is worth fighting for."

"So, what you're really saying is I need to stop hiding out in this stall and make a battle plan." If only she knew where to start.

Brody rocked his head side to side. "Never said that. Hiding has its merits. Sometimes. Other times, you have to cowboy up."

"Get back in the saddle after getting bucked off." Tenley rolled her eyes. "That's the metaphor you're going to use? Really?"

He tugged her ponytail. "Whatever works, little sister."

"I need to find Mac. If he's going to take Jade back to her house, then we should figure out some sort of schedule." She stood and brushed hay from her jeans. The mare shuffled forward a step, then another. Her low breath huffed over Tenley's arm, and she bumped her nose into Tenley's elbow. Tenley raised a hand to the swirl of hair in the center of the mare's forehead. "It's okay. You're safe here too. Even if you don't realize it yet."

"I think she's figuring it out." Brody stood and unlatched the door. He held it open for Tenley and closed and locked it behind them both. "I'll see you up at the house."

"Thanks, Brody." Tenley hugged her brother.

He didn't often allow displays such as this, but tonight, he held her tight, rocking them side to side. "Jade's fortunate to have you, and Mac will do what's right. He's hurting. Don't forget that he lost someone too."

Tenley stuffed the tears back to keep them from falling. Brody was right. She'd let her own emotions run rampant without real thought to how Mac must be feeling. She hurried from the barn and almost ran smack into Mac.

He reeled back, his hands gripping her arms to keep them from falling.

"I was just coming to find you." His voice held a gruffness that might mean anything.

Tenley let herself relax into his touch, knowing it wouldn't last.

Sure enough, he blinked once and then dropped his arms back to his sides. "Feel like arguing some more?" He said it with a hint of a teasing lilt. One side of his mouth quirked up, and he thumbed his hat back. Dusk had fallen an hour before, leaving the yard decorated in shadows.

Tenley bit back the immediate retort and focused on the darkness ringing his eyes, the way he constantly seemed to need to move. He rolled his shoulder again, the same one from before, and winced. The signs were obvious now that she took the time to look. Mac wasn't sleeping well. Grief sat on him with a crushing hold.

"I think it's good that you want to spend time with Jade at her old house." She let a beat of silence slip between them. "We can work this out, Mac. There are more options that neither of us have considered. You could stay here. Mom and Dad have a spare room."

He shook his head before she finished. "The whole point is to get to know my niece away from everyone else. I won't have your parents to lean on once we get to Chicago."

"Stop saying Chicago like it's the golden trophy at the end of the football season." She gripped the sides of her head and breathed in slow through her nose. "You've never taken care of Jade on your own. Maybe it would be an easier transition if you had people around to help at first." She wasn't giving into his idea of leaving Tama-rack Springs, but she had to attempt to get him to see that there was more involved than he'd considered.

His lips puckered into a frown.

Tenley forged ahead. "Why don't you let her stay here during the week? We already have a schedule in place that gets her to school on time. She can stay with you from Friday after school until Sunday night. As long as you bring her here for her riding classes on Friday and Saturday, and church on Sunday."

"You make it sound like we're parents splitting custody after a divorce."

She winced at the tone and the implication but kept her mouth shut tight.

Mac needed time to consider her proposal. She knew him well enough to remember that he hated feeling pushed into anything. He considered every angle. He did things by the book. He did the right thing even when it was hard. Even when it hurt him. They were alike in that regard, even if he didn't know it.

He angled his head to the side, peering at Tenley as thoughts scattered across his expression like pieces of broken glass. She'd done that to him, broken him and left him to put the pieces back together on his own.

"Okay." His voice was a mere whisper. He took off his hat and tilted his head to the stars appearing overhead. "I'll be here every day after school. Every lesson. If she's not at school, I'll be with her. I'll pick her up on Friday."

"And bring her for her lessons?" Tenley reiterated her demands.

Mac nodded. Lines fanned out from his eyes when his expression tightened. "And church on Sunday."

Tenley held out her hand.

Mac looked at it like he expected her to slap him, but soon enough his callused palm slid against hers. He shook it once, then let go and stepped back.

Tenley curled her fingers together as the memory of his touch lingered.

Chapter Seven

Mac picked up Jade after her equine therapy session Friday after school and took her straight to her old house. She lingered on the edge of the porch, her unicorn backpack slung over her shoulder and a frown tugging her mouth down as she sank her teeth into her lip.

"It's okay." Mac held out a hand. "Take your time." He should give her an out. Tell her that she didn't have to go inside, but he hesitated. What if she refused to stay? How was this going to work? He'd never spent time alone with Jade unless it was a couple hours while Amber and her husband went out to dinner, while Jade and Mac vegged out in his Chicago apartment, watching TV.

Zeus pushed his head against Jade's other side. She gripped the ruff around his neck with her free hand and lowered her head.

Mac waited. He knew how to be patient when it really mattered. Tenley shattered his senses, but patience remained for Jade.

Jade's grip tightened around his fingers. She gulped and took a step forward. Zeus moved with her, keeping pace with his head pressed tight to her stomach. He took up the protective stance that he usually only awarded to Mac.

The dog was one in a million. Mac let Jade set the

pace. They stepped into the house and he blinked to let his eyes adjust. After spending the last few days cleaning and restocking with essentials, he knew what she'd see. The small living room held a couch and a recliner nestled along the back wall. A small TV was mounted on the opposite wall, and a rectangular coffee table was pushed into the middle of the room.

The kitchen lay on the other side of the living room, a straight shot from the front door. Jade glanced that way before angling her steps to the short hallway to the right of the front door. The hallway led to two bedrooms and one bathroom. Jade's old room came up, the first door on the left.

She stopped in the open doorway. The buttery yellow walls melded into the soft pastel pink of Jade's bed, with its matching nightstand and toy chest. Pictures of horses and puppies hung haphazardly on the walls with strips of tape.

Jade's hand spasmed, and Mac watched her grip and release the thick fur on Zeus's neck. The dog scoured the room, searching it for any hint of danger. The instinct Mac had honed in the dog refused to rest, even now.

It's what made them such a great team…until he'd gotten them shot. His shoulder ached as though to remind him of what happened when he didn't follow the rules.

"Where's my stuff?" Jade let go of his hand and moved toward the bed. Her steps slowed, and she ran a hand over the freshly washed cover. "My stuffed animals are missing."

"They're in the basket in your closet." Mac pulled open the sliding door, revealing the pink laundry basket stuffed to overflowing.

Jade shook her head. "They don't go there. They go on

the bed. Mama…" She sniffed and wiped her nose with her sleeve. "Mama always kept them on the bed for me." She lifted her chin and spared Mac a glance before grabbing the basket. She grunted and hauled it toward the bed.

Mac's heart faltered, pain piercing deep.

"Do you want me to help?" He clenched and unclenched his hands. He longed to leap in and do it for her, but the jut of her chin and the sudden glint of stubbornness warned him away. He still couldn't resist asking.

Jade grunted again and pulled the basket while walking backward. "I got it."

Zeus whined while keeping up his position beside her.

Mac ran a hand through his hair, feeling the way the buzzed sides had grown out since he came back. "Okay. I'll go make us a snack, then." He backed into the hallway still watching, feeling helpless. "Call out if you need me."

"'Kay." Jade managed to drag the basket all the way to the side of the bed. She grabbed a stuffed dog from the top of the pile and placed it right on top of her pillow. She reached for another, and a tear trickled down her cheek. She sniffed it back and shoved the stuffed lion beside the dog. Her movements turned jerky, almost angry, as she moved one stuffed animal at a time.

He was in over his head. He knew that now. He'd expected the house would have an impact on Jade. He'd expected a few tears. He'd not considered that Jade hadn't yet reached the anger stage of her grief process. Not that grief was in any way a linear process. Did children even work through anger the same as adults? That was Tenley's specialty. He'd seen her in action with that little boy, Cody. He shook his head, worried. Jade might've processed her anger, only for her old home to bring it back when she confronted the familiar space. Maybe he'd been right when he told Tenley that Jade could use a fresh start in a new place.

He crossed to the foot of Jade's bed and sat down on the floor. She might want to do this on her own, but that didn't mean he had to leave her to go through this by herself. He'd stay as long as she needed. Mac stretched out his legs and crossed his ankles. Jade shot him a look but kept up her frenzied pace of returning every stuffed animal to the bed. He'd not known what to do with them. When he first came into her room, they'd been strewn around the floor, the bed rumpled with sheets and blankets tossed aside, like Jade had left in a hurry.

He should ask Tenley what happened that day. His throat convulsed. He knew the basics of Amber's crash, but not the minute details. He knew Jade was not in the car with her parents. Had she been here? With who? Tenley? Why? The questions kept coming, piling up on him until he couldn't bear the weight anymore.

Jade finished her mission, returning the gray-and-white stuffed horse last. She tucked it into the pile and stroked its mane. "He's the last one. Daddy bought him for my birthday." She sniffed again. "He said he'd buy me a real horse when I turn eight." Her chin lifted. She dragged her hands down her cheeks, scrubbing away the last of the tears. "Can we have spaghetti for supper?"

"Sure." He'd agree to almost anything at this point. He pushed to his feet and held out his hand. Her resilience humbled him.

Jade chewed on her bottom lip, then grabbed the stuffed horse from the bed and hugged it to her chest with one arm while she grabbed hold of his hand with the other. "Can I feed Zeus?"

"Absolutely. And after dinner, we'll take him into the

backyard and play fetch." He squeezed her hand. "Would you like that?"

"What about Rascal? Can we bring him here too? Zeus likes him, and I want to show him the house." Her green eyes pleaded with him. She'd lost so much in her short life.

How could he ask her to give up more? Which meant he'd be taking a little girl, her rambunctious puppy and his old man, Zeus, home to Chicago. Throat tight, he dipped his chin to his chest. "We'll bring him back tomorrow after your riding lesson."

Jade let go of his hand and walked ahead of him. She climbed onto a kitchen chair and crossed her arms on the tabletop.

What was he doing here? Mac faced away from the curiosity burning in Jade's eyes. He dove into preparing the meal, like making spaghetti was the most important mission in the world. Right now, it was. Nothing else mattered except helping Jade get through this. One meal at a time, if that's what it took.

He worried about the other details as he cooked pasta and mixed up a quick recipe for homemade sauce. The day-to-day of raising his niece felt real after they finished eating and she helped him clear the table. His hours with the Chicago PD were a complication he'd put aside. He needed someone to watch Jade while he worked. Someone to keep her safe when she wasn't at school in the summer and when he worked weekends. Sheriff Hanks popped into Mac's thoughts. The sheriff had mentioned a job. That he'd like to have Mac back at the department.

Staying in Tamarack Springs solved so many problems. All but one, really. But that one—the one that took up a Tenley-shaped space in his heart—couldn't be overlooked.

Mac carried their empty dishes to the sink and wiped

his hands. "Come on. We'll go outside while there's still light." He'd worry about dishes—and everything else— once Jade fell asleep.

They stepped out into a brisk May wind. An approaching storm tinged the air with hints of rain. Fading sunlight dappled the yard and filtered through the many oaks that lined the far side of the picket fence. Mac handed Jade a tennis ball. "Why don't you throw it for him?" He made a hand motion at Zeus, but the dog already had his attention riveted on Jade and the ball in her hand.

Jade raced to the middle of the yard and hurled the ball toward the back of the fence.

Zeus streaked after it, belly low to the ground. The exercise was good for him and would keep him in shape for when he returned to work. *If.* If Zeus returned to work. Mac looked the dog over with a critical eye. He still had a few years of police work in him, if his captain agreed.

That was the crux of the matter. Mac still hadn't heard back about his administrative leave being lifted. When the captain asked if Mac thought he'd made the right call, while he lay in the hospital bed bandaged and sore to the very marrow of his bones, Mac didn't have an answer. He still didn't.

Maybe that was the problem. He spent his life following the rules and controlling every aspect of his life. Until the moment when he knew his partner was in danger and he'd flung all his training aside to save the man's life.

It was only by God's grace that Mac and Zeus had lived through the assault.

And he couldn't bring himself to be sorry for breaking protocol. A fact his captain must've recognized when he asked Mac to walk him through what happened. Weren't rules sometimes meant to be broken when the outcome of that choice seemed less than perfect?

Given the same choices, Mac would do it all again.

Thunder rumbled overhead. Tree branches swayed, the wind whipping them into a frenzy. Jade stiffened, her shoulders drawing up to her ears. She bolted for the porch and threw herself at his legs. "I want to go home."

"You are home." He patted the back of her head. "Are you afraid of the thunder?"

She nodded once, her entire body trembling.

Zeus raced around the yard, barking at the darkening sky. Lightning zigzagged through the clouds in brilliant purple streaks. Mac narrowed his eyes against the glare. Thunder cracked nearby, and Jade screamed.

Zeus ran for the house and slammed into Jade. He planted his paws on her feet and pushed his head into her side.

"Let's go inside." Mac held the door for Jade.

She loosened her grip on his leg and wrapped her arms around Zeus's neck. They hurried into the house. Jade hesitated at the kitchen table, her eyes darting around fearfully. "Can we go back?" Her voice quivered.

"Back where?" He spread his hands as confusion overtook him. "We're safe inside. The storm can't get us here."

As though to argue with him, the house shook with the next boom of thunder. Lightning crashed at the same time, illuminating the kitchen in a blinding flash.

Jade clapped her hands over her ears. "I want to go home."

Mac dropped to a knee, bringing them eye level. "I don't understand. Jade, you are home."

She shook her head and threw her arms around his neck. "Not this home. Tenley's home. I want Aunt Tenley."

He scooped Jade into a hug, and her head dropped onto his shoulder. "I won't let anything happen to you."

"I'm scared, Uncle Mac."

"I know, baby." He was too. Not about the storm. He loved the crispness of the air during a good one. The raging, untamable power that surged and seemed to fill the sky. He saw God in the wildness. He kissed the top of Jade's head and stood, carrying her to the couch where he settled in with Jade tight to his side. "Why are you afraid of the storm?"

He didn't remember her being afraid before. She used to sit with him in Chicago and watch it rain. Though the storms there were nothing like this.

Zeus stretched out across Mac's feet, his head on his paws. Jade nestled in close, her hands cradled under her chin. She implored Mac with her gaze. "I don't want to stay here." The quick plea broke Mac's heart.

He couldn't deny her. What kind of monster would he be to insist that she stayed?

"Let's make sure Tenley is home. Okay?" He pulled his phone from his pocket and tapped Tenley's contact button. Thank goodness he'd thought to get the information from her earlier.

Tenley answered on the first ring. "Everything okay?"

He wanted to lash out that he was perfectly capable of taking care of Jade. But was he? Really? He'd managed a handful of hours before Jade wanted to go back to Tenley. Maybe it was just the storm. But what if it was more? Mac gritted his teeth until he gained control. "Jade wants to come back to your house. She doesn't like the weather."

"If you leave now, you should be able to stay ahead of the rain. The front door is open." Tenley spoke quickly and without admonishment or scorn. "I'll be waiting for you."

Those last five words punched straight through him, hitting harder than the bullet that ripped through his shoulder and punctured his lung. He couldn't breathe for several heartbeats as her words settled around him. He'd told her that same thing the night before their wedding. He'd held her close and kissed her until nothing else mattered but the two of them and the hopes of forever.

He ended the call without saying goodbye, then patted Jade's back. "Grab what you need."

She leaped from the couch and sprinted toward her room. Mac was still pulling on his boots when she returned with her backpack over one shoulder and two more stuffed animals in her hands. "Zeus too?"

"Yep. We'll bring him too." Mac whistled for Zeus, and the dog lumbered to his feet with a long stretch and a yawn. Mac checked the weather through the living room window. "Okay. It's not raining yet. You go straight to the truck while I lock the door."

Jade sank her teeth into her bottom lip. "Zeus will go with me?"

"Of course." Mac pushed the front door open against the howling wind. Any other time, he'd avoid driving in weather like this. It wasn't safe. But Jade's mental state couldn't handle that argument. He hurried to lock the door and followed Jade to the truck. He helped her inside, then closed the door behind Zeus.

The drive to Tenley's passed quickly, the wind pushing them from behind, rocking the truck. Mac kept both hands on the wheel and his jaw locked. Jade held on to Zeus with a white-knuckled grip until they pulled up in front of Tenley's little house on the Jacobs' ranch. Her pumpkin-orange door stood out in the darkness, a beacon of comfort to the dreary night.

Tenley opened the door and stood limned in the brightness behind her. She ran for his truck. Jade fumbled with her seat, once Mac killed the engine. He heaved against the wind and hurried around the truck, shielding Tenley from the gusting breeze.

Jade leaped into Tenley's arms, wrenching a new knot in Mac's heart.

"Come on." Tenley grabbed a fistful of his shirt and pulled, hauling him toward the house.

"I should go." He dug in his heels.

"No." Tenley and Jade shouted together amid a long rumble of thunder.

Jade pleaded over Tenley's shoulder. "You have to stay with me."

The knot in his throat threatened to strangle him right then and there. Tenley kept hold of his shirt, pulling him forward despite the sudden woodenness of his legs.

He followed her into the house, Zeus at his heels. The dog stopped inside the threshold and eyed the new space. Mac palmed the door shut as another gust came howling down the mountain.

Lightning flickered and danced through the windows. Mac blinked to clear his vision and to adjust to the brightness. Tenley had every light blazing. Lanterns lined the counter in the kitchen to his left. They were unlit but ready, along with four flashlights.

"I made hot chocolate." Tenley scraped her long, dark curls from her face after lowering Jade to the floor. The sight of her hair undone from its usual braid or ponytail pulled at his attention. She smiled, and Mac noted the tightness around her eyes. "It's going to be okay, Jade. Rascal is in the laundry room. You can let him out if it's okay with Mac and Zeus."

Zeus whined while looking at Mac like he understood the words, then padded quickly toward a white door.

"I think Zeus would like that." Mac scrubbed his palms along his thighs to rid them of the longing to reach out for Tenley.

She still held his shirt in one fisted hand. When she took a step toward the kitchen, the sudden pull of resistance snapped her head around. She flushed bright red and snatched her hand back. A quick shake of her head and she rubbed her thumb across her palm. "Sorry." She cleared her throat and took another step backward. "Want some hot chocolate?"

No. He wanted her. He wanted to rewind the years. He wanted to know what had happened between them. He wanted a second chance to be her forever. That last one rocked him onto his heels as he realized the truth digging past his resolve. It snapped and crackled brighter than the lightning outside.

Something had gone horribly wrong seven years ago. Could he forgive what she was so unwilling to reveal? The secret her family staunchly protected too? Or would it harden his heart against her—against them—like she so feared?

He followed her into the kitchen, still reeling from the epiphany pulling him back and forth. Tenley poured three cups of hot chocolate from a pot on the stove. She passed him one and took the other. "I'll let Jade's cool for a bit. The dogs should keep her busy."

"Why doesn't she like storms?" Mac sipped the blistering hot beverage, scalding his tongue and keeping him from asking the questions battering against the walls he'd erected around his heart.

Tenley's heart-rending sigh and the sudden shine of

tears in her eyes completely brought down his defenses. What had he unbottled with that question? He lowered the cup and reached for her. His body moved with the aching quickness of muscle memory. The need to comfort her rose above all others. She settled into his embrace, and it was like the pieces that shattered years ago snugged back into place.

"We found out about Amber during a storm. They were coming home from a dinner date in Bridgeport." She whispered the tragedy between thundering booms.

Mac's body tensed and relaxed in waves. "The report said they wrecked after hitting a deer."

"They did." Tenley nodded, her cheek scratching the thick cotton of his shirt. "The storm came after. It's why it took so long for anyone to notice the accident."

His cheek landed on top of her head. He held her tighter, rocking them both side to side as grief welled. It ebbed and flowed, rushing through him in a torrent. Outside, the thunder abated, but his tears finally flooded free. The thunder and lightning rolled into the mountains after lashing the windows with rain. It fell now in soft sheets that peppered the tin roof overhead and created a gentle symphony.

Storms in the mountains were like that. They blew in, furious and bent on destruction, only to calm and beguile with rain-tinged air.

"I'm sorry, Mac." Tenley cried into his shirt too. Her arms snaked around his waist and gripped the back of his shirt. "I'm so sorry."

He heard more than one apology in the agony of her voice. "Me too." It was the best he could do. After another heartbeat of the blessed torture of holding Tenley, he let go.

Jade scampered into the kitchen. Zeus and Rascal bounded behind her, ears flopping. Zeus sat and eyed Mac, his head tipped to the side. Rascal copied Zeus after giving the older dog a quick look. Rascal's oversize white ears stood straight up, turning his expression comical when the pup opened his mouth and his tongue lolled out.

"Here." Tenley held out Jade's hot chocolate, sniffing back tears. "Sit at the table and drink this. Then we'll get you ready for bed."

Mac checked the clock, surprised to see the lateness of the hour. Adrenaline continued to pump through his system, and he knew he wouldn't sleep much tonight.

He stood back and let Tenley take over Jade's care. She didn't seem to mind their obvious tears. Maybe they'd been doing a lot of crying together, which was probably a good thing. He felt better than he had in months.

He finished his drink and poured another from the pot, then topped off Tenley's cup while she ushered Jade down the hallway. Their voices filtered out, both quiet and Jade seemingly calm now that the storm had abated.

It might no longer flash outside, but Mac felt it start up again inside him. The storm gathered and surged through him. Try as he might, he couldn't escape the gravity of what lay ahead. The decisions to be made. The reality of having a little girl. The responsibility he bore to his sister. Jade couldn't even make it through the night without Tenley. Maybe it was the storm. Maybe not. What would happen if he *did* take Jade to Chicago? Tenley couldn't save him then.

Suddenly, leaving all this behind a second time didn't appeal as much as before. He'd settled back into this place. Chicago never felt like home. The closest he'd come was when he married Laura. Without her there, it was just another place.

Tenley returned, her arms burdened down with blankets and pillows. "You can sleep on the couch." She pointed her chin at the plush brown couch that curved around the corner of the living room.

"I should go back to Amber's." He couldn't call it home. If anything, this place—Tenley's place—felt more like home than anywhere he'd been in a long time.

"Don't." Tenley sighed and tossed the blankets onto the couch behind him. "Jade made me promise that you'd be here when she woke up." A disconcerting look crossed her face. She hugged her elbows tight over her abdomen. "I need to go to the library in the morning for Saturday's book reading. Jade wants to stay here with you."

"Did you promise that too?" His voice came out too harsh. Old habits died hard when confronted with one of Tenley's promises.

Tenley pushed her fingers into her eyes and sat on the coffee table. "No. I said I'd ask you." She motioned at the door. "If you want to leave, go ahead. I'll explain to Jade in the morning." Her shoulders rounded, with what he couldn't say. Disappointment. Frustration. Fatigue. Any manner of things might weigh on Tenley. Things he no longer had the right to ask about.

But he wanted to. He almost asked her right then why she'd walked away. Earlier this week, in the barn, it had felt like she wanted to explain. Maybe it was time he found out the truth. If he heard her say the words, heard her say she'd stopped loving him, then he could move on.

Except she'd said on the trail ride that she'd never stopped loving him. Confusion warred within him.

He dropped onto the edge of the couch and leaned his elbows on his knees.

Zeus sat pressed into Mac's leg. Rascal raced around the coffee table. He zipped left and right, happiness radiating from his puppy face. He ran himself into exhaustion, then collapsed on Tenley's socked feet. She ruffled the pup's ears, and he thought he heard another sigh before she lifted her head. "Mac." His name whispered between them, drawing him into the lullaby sound of her voice.

He lurched to his feet. "I'm going to check on Jade." Almost running, he retreated to the room where he'd seen Tenley and Jade go.

Jade lay on a twin bed, a pink blanket pulled under her chin and her stuffed animals in a row along the wall.

He dropped to his knees beside the bed and started to take Jade's hand. She grunted and rolled over, her frown and the whoosh of a quiet cry threatening to ruin the tiny morsel of peace he'd taken from this place. He rolled to his feet and brushed a kiss over the top of her head before backtracking to the living room where Tenley sat in the same position.

She didn't look up, barely moved. She remained so still that he wondered if she'd fallen asleep.

He angled his steps toward the kitchen, and Tenley's quiet steps followed him. They sat across from each other at the kitchen table, the harsh fluorescent light highlighting the hollowness of Tenley's cheeks.

He drummed his fingers on the table, the sound echoing the quiet rainfall pattering against the windows.

"I'm sorry. For everything." How many times would it take hearing her say "I'm sorry" for him to believe her? Tenley knotted her fingers together on the tabletop. Her gaze skirted his, never landing on anything. "If you want to hear it, I'll try and explain why I did what I did."

His heartbeat picked up the refrain between needing to know and refusing to allow Tenley any quarter. She already took up too much space in his thoughts. "Will it change anything between us now?"

"Probably." Tenley winced. "If by change you mean make things worse."

His heart fell.

Worse. "I can't handle worse, Ten." The nickname came against his bidding. It slipped into the quiet between them. Mac propped his head up in his hands and closed his eyes. "I'm barely making it day by day. I don't know what to do about Jade. My job. Chicago. I had a plan, and now I don't know what to do." He allowed the truth freedom to roam. Tenley made it easy to confess his insecurities. She always had, because she never judged him for them. She helped him understand himself in a way no one else ever had.

"Have you prayed about it?"

The question surprised him, and his head jerked in response. "God and I are not exactly speaking to each other."

"On the contrary, I don't think He stopped talking to you. Maybe you quit listening." She unknotted her fingers and stretched out one hand toward him. "God doesn't run away when we throw a temper tantrum."

"You think that's what I'm doing? You think I'm a toddler who's pitching a fit over the fact that he's lost everyone he's ever loved?" He scoffed, the sound lodging between them.

Tenley took his hand. The shock of it slammed into him. His fingers curled around hers despite his orders to let her go. His head and his heart fought each other, and his heart won when his hand tightened. The grip had to hurt, but Tenley never flinched. She simply wrapped her other hand over his and held on tight.

"You didn't lose everyone." Her throat convulsed in an audible swallow. "I'm still here."

Was she saying what he thought?

He couldn't handle that either.

"I need to focus on Jade and what she needs. Everything else—" he waved between them "—all this. It will have to wait. Our past has waited this long. It can wait a while longer. Jade is all that matters. I have to do what's right by Jade."

"Then, stay." Tenley pursed her lips and blinked furiously. "I'm sorry." She lifted her chin. "Wait. No, I'm not. This is what Jade needs. This place. The people here. She's comfortable here and is surrounded with people who love her. What will she have in Chicago?"

"Me." He forced aside the guilt and focused on the woman across from him. She'd grown up. His fiancée Tenley loved arguing, but she was reckless. This version had a wisdom that he'd never expected. "You think I'm not enough for her?"

"Don't put words in my mouth." Tenley shot him a look that pierced him to the bone. "What about your job?" Tenley's grip on his hands never faltered. "We have a system here that works. Jade is always with someone she knows. She has her therapy here, the horses."

Mac pulled his hands free of Tenley. "You're not the only one who loves her. And you're not the only one who can take care of her." He took a slow breath to steady his pulse and his racing thoughts. Everything Tenley said made sense. Was he being stubborn out of a need to hurt Tenley? Was he that far gone?

He searched his heart, and for the first time, he saw all of his actions since coming back with a clarity he'd been missing. He'd thwarted Tenley at every turn because he didn't want to trust her with Jade. She'd hurt him, and he wanted her to feel that pain.

He stared into the abyss of his heart and didn't like what he saw waiting for him there. He saw loneliness and a desire for revenge. Tenley had pegged him from day one.

His lungs tightened, constricting his next breath. Mac ran a palm down his face and groaned.

Tenley shifted, almost rising before he stopped her with an upraised hand. She settled back in her seat. "You'll think about what I said?"

The fact that she read him so easily after all these years should be disconcerting. He shifted in his seat and massaged his forehead. "I'll think about it."

She stood and moved around the table. Mac tensed in preparation, but she merely patted his shoulder and moved on. "I'll see you in the morning."

He wanted to collapse right here on the kitchen floor as the fatigue slammed into him. Instead, he shoved to his feet and stumbled to the couch where he removed his boots and kicked them under the table. He tossed a sheet over the couch and face-planted onto the stack of pillows while dragging a blanket over his shoulders. He expected to stay awake, his thoughts in turmoil, but seconds after his head hit the pillow, the gently tapping rain lulled him to sleep.

Chapter Eight

Children giggled as Tenley gathered them into a loose semicircle for Saturday Book Nook. Tamarack Springs's local library believed in helping kids read, and Miss Williams, the librarian, welcomed the parade of readers from her place behind the curved desk where she'd been librarian for as long as Tenley could remember. The rambunctious children's voices were enough to make Tenley offer her an apologetic smile.

Tenley had left Jade with Mac at her house—a house that, last night, Jade had called *home*.

Tenley swallowed and focused. "Who's ready for a story?" She slipped around the edge of the group, grinning at the upturned faces. "I thought we'd read one of my favorites."

"Me." Their voices chorused together, creating a unique blend that Tenley adored.

Cool air ruffled hair on several small heads, and hands clapped intermittently when Tenley picked up her dog-eared edition of *The Tale of Peter Rabbit*.

"Will you do the voices?" Angelina popped onto her knees.

"She aways does the voices, Angewina." Peter's lisp swapped *l*'s for *w*'s. His head cocked to the side, reminding Tenley of a cocker spaniel when brown curls drooped over his ears.

Mattie threw his arms around Peter. "Will you be Peter? You're such a good hopper."

The seventy-year-old Miss Williams shook her head at Mattie and Peter, but a smile teased the edges of her stern expression. Fast friends since the day they met last year, the two boys loved interactive story time.

Tenley sat in the oversize red rocking chair as a dozen pairs of eyes locked on to her. Opening the book with reverence, in a low, mysterious voice, she began. "'Once upon a time, there were four little Rabbits...'" When she reached Peter's name, the human Peter hopped around the group, eliciting a round of giggles and clapping.

For the next hour, Peter and the others alternated acting out bits while she read. Before she knew it, parents arrived to pick up their littles. Miss Williams stood and braced her hands on the desk. "Excellent reading, as always. Same time next week?"

Every Saturday morning for the last year, Miss Williams ended story time with the same question. Tenley smiled at the blessed routine. She'd started coming here after her first year of sobriety, a way to make amends or to help in some small way.

"Sure thing." Tenley tightened her grip on her bag. "I'll see you next week."

"I've been meaning to talk to you about a summer program." Miss Williams nudged her glasses up her nose, rattling the silver chain that allowed them to dangle around her neck when not in use. "All of the elementary school is participating in a reading program, and I wanted to ensure that Jade will be joining her class."

Tenley gulped air and tried to force words through the

sudden tightness in her throat. She didn't dare mention
the situation between her and Mac. Her stomach knotted.
She still had time. If she could get him to fall in love with
Tamarack Springs again, maybe moving back to Chicago
would lose its luster. If they could be friends, maybe she
wouldn't have to lose Jade too. Her hands clenched into
fists. A week of being face-to-face with Mac shouldn't
have her feeling this strongly about him. But wishing he
might fall in love with more than the town was the most
wishful of thinking.

At least he'd implied he'd try to be friends. That had
to be enough. Nothing more. She could never run the risk
of hurting him like that ever again. He deserved better.

Slinging the bag crossways over her chest, Tenley pulled
the door open. "I'll do my best to make sure Jade is here."

Miss Williams held the door behind Tenley. "It's a good
thing you're doing for that girl. Not everyone has someone willing to step in when they're needed."

Tenley resisted the urge to argue. She was doing her
best for Jade. Even though it felt like nothing she did
was ever enough to make up for the mistakes in her past.
God had forgiven her. And she'd done her best to forgive
herself. Even Brody, Molly and their parents held no ill
will against Tenley. None they mentioned, though she
felt their assessing looks following her around the ranch
every time she fell into a foul mood. Like she might bolt
at any moment. There had been a few close calls in those
early years, but not in a long, long time. She had all the
tools to keep her sobriety, and a million reasons to never
fall back into that pit.

Enough.

Tenley pushed the thoughts aside and focused on the
next task. Brody had texted her on her way into town,

asking if she'd help him with a new project involving the horses. She needed to get back to the ranch before he changed his mind or did it himself. Brody asking for help was another new development in her brother since Callie's return. Gone was the reticent cowboy who snarled at everyone who offered to ease the burdens he carried.

Tenley liked this version of her brother. He was still gruff and tough, but with a softer side that she'd not seen since they were in high school. He was proof people could change.

First, work with Brody and the horses. Then an afternoon with Mac as he hovered while Jade rode. Tenley shook her head at Mac's obstinacy. Why did he struggle with releasing even a smidgen of control?

If she wanted the brainpower to work through that mess, she needed breakfast.

She left her car parked outside Granny's. An empty sidewalk boded well for a quick sit-down. Inside the building, Tenley wove her way to the booth she'd shared with Mac throughout the years. She settled in and scanned the room before turning her attention out the window.

Pink and orange streaks spread across the sky in a fan of color among the dark clouds, their rays reaching with broad beams toward a small, nondescript building hunkering between two elaborate structures. With clapboard siding and an old green metal roof, it looked like the last century had forgotten the quaint structure. A closer look revealed stained-glass windows. Windows that had kept her busy for hours as a child. She'd imagined the building to be a castle, with a princess and a dragon. The windows were the key to a puzzle and only the bravest knight would earn the right to enter.

A longing to collapse onto a pew and trace the pat-

terns of light with her fingertips seeped in and drowned
out the cafe's noise, until Granny's voice sliced through
the daydream. "Mercy, girl, you're as lost in thought as
snow in Hawaii."

Granny bounced onto the seat across from Tenley and
patted her hands. "Tell Granny what's got you staring at
that old church."

"Who made the windows?" Okay. That wasn't what
she wanted to know. "I mean, if I went over there, are the
doors locked?" Open mouth. Insert foot. Tenley forced her
mouth to remain shut.

Like Miss Williams, Granny gave Tenley a quiet look
that read and assessed a wealth of information, all while
making her feel like a misbehaving child. "That place ain't
never locked. You go on and visit anytime. If ole Vernon
gives you any trouble, you tell him Granny said it's okay."

"I don't have time today." Tenley fiddled with the napkin on the table.

"Everyone always in such a rush." Granny huffed.
"Take it from an old woman, nothing changes by hurry-
ing through life." She waved a hand. "Pish. Listen to me
scold you like you're one of my own. Comes with watching you grow up here." She patted Tenley's hand again.
"Things have a way of sticking around here. People too.
Just give them a chance. Remind them of the good."

Was she talking about Mac? Tenley's cheeks burned,
and she knew they had to be bright red. She looked away
from Granny. "Some people can't change the hurt they
caused."

"No. But the good Lord says we ought to forgive them.
No one is the same today as they were years ago. We age,
we change. Sometimes, those changes are for the better."

She stood with a creak of old bones and held out her arms. "Give me a hug and I'll get your breakfast."

"You sure know how to bribe your customers." Tenley complied, allowing the comfort offered to do its job.

"Oh, child. You get as old as me, you learn a thing or two about people." She waved her hands around her head. "Most of them are so busy, they don't know which way they're going. The rest so still and quiet, the world passes them right by and they never notice. You got to learn to live in peace. Move forward and don't look back. Keep your eyes on God and He will make sure your path goes the right way."

Tenley cast a glance out the window, an undeniable tug drawing her back. No time today for a visit. She had a lesson to teach and horses to train.

Mac approached the round pen with cautious steps and peered through a gap in the vertical wooden slats. An obstacle course obstructed his view, the gates and poles not making sense to his untrained eye. He shifted to the side.

Tenley stood on the back of a horse, her arms spread wide.

Mac staggered to a halt, afraid to make a sound or movement. If the horse spooked… It didn't bear thinking. What was Tenley thinking to put herself at risk like this? His own conscience pricked. He had no right to judge her actions. Not after the way he barreled through his job, throwing himself into every dangerous situation like it didn't matter if he lived or not. Until Amber's death, it hadn't mattered.

Brody shuffled his boots in the dirt and led another horse into the ring. He lined the new horse's nose up with the tail of Tenley's mount. "Go ahead."

With the grace of a ballet dancer, Tenley stepped from one broad back to another. She spun, dancing her way from saddle to saddle before ending with one boot on either horse. Neither horse moved.

Mac's muscles relaxed when she jumped to the ground and praised both equines.

Brody cracked a smile and gave Tenley a nod. She beamed in response, a smile brighter than sunshine.

"Take her through." Brody handed her the reins to his horse, a blood bay. The horse tossed its head and chomped the bit.

Tenley swung aboard and clucked her tongue.

The first obstacle, a simple gate, presented no problems. But the second, a narrow beam that required patience and trust, caused the mare to halt and paw the strip of wood. Tenley sat relaxed in the saddle and asked the mare to move forward.

Hoof by hoof, the horse responded until they clomped off the other end. The mare gave a little buck. Tenley laughed and patted her neck.

They finished the course without further incident. Once Tenley started back toward Brody, Mac eased through the gate.

Tenley waved at him as she dismounted and jogged over. "Sorry. We're running a little late."

"You're helping Brody." Captain Obvious returned for another round. Mac rolled his head, dislodging the thought, and hoped Tenley didn't notice the tightness in his voice.

She unleashed the power of her smile. "He didn't intend for me to help. He asked Molly first. But she couldn't because she had to make a wedding cake. He let me, even though he wasn't happy at first." A glance at her brother, and her brows pressed over her eyes. "He might not be happy now, but he hasn't been a total brat."

So it was one of those days between the elder and middle siblings where they bantered with an underlying current of tension.

Brody stroked the other horse's nose. "I never said you weren't welcome. I asked if you were sure you wanted to help."

"Same difference." Tenley crossed her arms. The mare shoved her nose into Tenley's back, knocking her forward.

"You need me to come back later?" Mac turned to leave.

Tenley grabbed his sleeve. "Why don't you help us? We could use the extra hands, then I'll help you work with Rascal before Jade's lesson." She scrunched her nose. "He's started chewing all my shoes."

Mac laughed. He couldn't help it. "He's a puppy. He needs lots of activity and stimulation to wear him out. Bored dogs create chaos. Especially dogs like him who're meant to work." He motioned at Zeus sitting outside the gate. "It took years to train Zeus. Nothing good comes without hard work."

Her sigh slipped between them. "Point taken." She tugged on his sleeve again. "Will you help? I want to bring Shadow out and start some groundwork. It'll be good for her to have exposure to more humans. And Brody has a few other horses to take across the obstacle course."

He wanted to ask why he should help her. It was a selfish thought, but it lingered. He'd taken Jade up to Peter and Margaret's house when Margaret asked for Jade's help packaging meals for a local elderly couple. She'd promised to have Jade back in time for her therapy session with Freckles.

The last thing he wanted to do was go back to Tenley's and wait. He'd woken up this morning disoriented but with a sense of homecoming that he still hadn't shaken. Being here ignited too many memories. All of them good, except the last, the day he'd left and sworn never to come back. Never say never.

He should've packed Jade's stuff the minute he woke up and took the girl back to Amber's house. It would have saved him this problem of getting close to Tenley again. She dragged him in, one hesitant step at a time. He'd watched her train horses before. He knew her powers of persuasion over the equine mind. He'd just never expected her to have that same power over him.

He took in a ragged breath and shoved a hand across his stubbled cheek and caught Brody's eye. "You're not planning on putting me on a wild horse, are you?"

"Would I do that?" Brody's grin spoke of years of pranks and made zero promises.

Mac tucked his thumbs into his belt. "Yes."

Brody guffawed. "Maybe when we were kids and I knew you could handle it." He strode over and clapped a hand to Mac's shoulder. "You're in good hands. All the horses I'm working today are in need of fine-tuning. Sale prospects for the ranch. I need them to be kid-friendly and game for anything the trail might throw their way."

Mac released the knot of tension gathering between his shoulders. "Okay."

"Great." Brody handed Mac the reins to a dun gelding. "This is Pepper. He's been around the course several times, but it's been a few weeks since I've ridden him. Just take him over all the obstacles. He's not a fan of the pool noo-dles." Brody waved at the contraption that looked something like a car wash with pool noodles sticking out on either side of a narrow tunnel. "Take it slow."

Mac gathered up the reins, checked his girth and lowered the stirrups to the length he needed, then swung into the saddle. Pepper snorted and shook his mane. "My thoughts exactly." Mac patted the horse's neck and clicked his tongue. The gelding responded and carried him forward across the wooden seesaw, barely hesitating when the structure shifted under the weight.

He heard Tenley and Brody behind him but focused on the horse. Pepper's steps shortened, his agitation showing in the way he pranced without making any real movement forward. The gelding eyed the pool noodles and sidestepped.

Mac kept pressure on with his heels, urging the horse forward and offering encouragement with continuous murmurs and pats to his neck. "Come on. You can do it. I know it looks scary. Looks like it might gobble you up, but it's safe. I wouldn't ask you to do anything that would hurt you."

Hadn't the pastor preached on something similar last week? That God was there through every trial, even when it felt like He'd abandoned His children. Mac's grip on the reins tightened, and the gelding responded with another sidestep.

"Easy now." Mac guided him back to the tunnel and waited. "Hey, Tenley." He called softly over his shoulder.

"Yeah?" She jogged over.

"Do me a favor and walk through there." Mac nudged his chin at the tunnel. "Let him see what happens. Better yet, lead that other horse through first."

"You got it." Tenley hurried away, her steps sending puffs of dust billowing up to sparkle in the sunlight. She came back within seconds, leading the bay horse. She never slowed as she walked into the tunnel. The horse followed without a fuss.

Pepper's ears flicked, swiveling from Mac to the horse and back.

Tenley reappeared at the other end.

"Now, lead him back through, coming toward us." Underneath Mac, Pepper shifted. The tightness eased from the gelding's muscles when his friend came back through the tunnel unscathed.

Tenley stopped the horse nose to nose with Pepper. She glanced up at him, a smile brimming. "Go on, Pepper."

Mac nudged, and the horse responded, walking between the rows of pool noodles like he'd done it every single day. Mac repeated the path several more times, until Pepper didn't hesitate at all.

Tenley watched from the edge of the round pen, her arms crossed with the reins looped between them. She propped one booted foot on the wall behind her. "You should consider training horses with Brody."

"Not my job experience." He swung from the saddle and rubbed Pepper's forehead. "I just know what it's like to face a path that seems impossible and know that you have no choice but to go through it. Even when it looks like you'll never come out the other end unscathed."

"Mac—" Tenley started his way.

Mac held up a hand to stop her. "It's okay. You did what you had to do. I survived." Seemed like he kept surviving. He wished he knew why. What was God's plan? What was the end goal in all this? This pain? What purpose did it serve? "Now I have to do what I need to do, and I need you to give me the space to find my way."

She pursed her lips and kept silent. It stretched between them, taut as a barbed wire fence. "I understand what you're saying. But you also don't have all the details. You don't know all the pitfalls that were laid in your path. When you're ready…" She took a shaky breath. "If you want to know why I did it, I'll tell you."

"Soon." Mac promised while leading Pepper away. "Not yet, but soon." He couldn't believe all the answers he wanted were a breath away, and yet his heart railed against hearing it. He'd have to deal with the truth sooner or later. No matter how painful it might be. But fear had an iron grip on reasoning.

When it first happened, he'd been too hurt and angry. He'd demanded answers, and when she didn't give them—didn't answer his calls or even come to see him—he'd left it all behind. But like most things, the not knowing ate at him. For every time he said it didn't matter, that Tenley did what she did and he'd gotten over it, there were moments when all he wanted was the truth.

Why had the woman he'd loved with his entire being pushed him aside like yesterday's garbage? He'd promised from the day they met to protect her. He'd never expected that he'd need to protect himself from her.

Chapter Nine

Tenley walked alongside Mac, her arms swinging loosely by her sides. He stared straight ahead. She'd expected a lot of anger from him after his arrival, and he'd fulfilled that. And more. But this felt like something else.

A weight had settled on him that wasn't there before. Every step seemed to be harder than the last. Tenley tried to shake off the feeling that it was her fault, but she knew the truth. All of this *was* her fault. Her dad's accident. Mac leaving Tamarack Springs. Even Amber's accident could be laid at Tenley's doorstep. She'd been the one to insist Amber and her husband needed a date night. She'd been the one to put it all together so the couple could enjoy dinner and a late movie while she watched Jade. The ache of that secret was hers alone to bear.

Her decisions were toxic to those she loved. Even decisions made while sober hurt those around her. How could she be trusted to take care of Jade when she continually hurt everyone?

She recoiled from the truth and forced her gaze ahead. Just because she wasn't worthy didn't mean she'd let Mac take Jade to Chicago. Jade deserved to make a life here, at a place she loved. Selfish. Tenley was being selfish.

She didn't want to give up her one link to Amber after losing Mac.

Mac lengthened his stride, and Tenley hurried to catch up. His reaction to the obstacle course in the round pen haunted her. His words swirled around, mixing with her guilt.

"What you said earlier, about the path not hurting…" She trailed off, uncertain what she really wanted to say.

Mac didn't slow. If anything, he sped up. His lips flattened into a thin line.

"I feel like everywhere I turn, I get hurt." Tenley forged ahead, feeling her way into the conversation. "No matter what I do, people I love get hurt." She winced against the painful words. Mac didn't care about her troubles anymore. She was just Troublesome Tenley, the middle Jacobs' sibling. The one everyone overlooked in favor of Brody the Brave and Molly the Magnificent. Okay, that was going too far. Tenley had no one to blame for her actions but herself. She knew that, but blaming her problems on other people was so much easier.

It hurt to know that she'd allowed those thoughts to drive her all those years ago. Back in high school when teachers compared her to her siblings, always with a tone that said Tenley was lacking. It stung. And it pushed her to be different. Only she'd chosen the wrong way to put an end to the pain of never measuring up.

Mac didn't respond, but she didn't expect him too. Mac took the idea of a "man of few words" to heart. Unless he was angry with her, which seemed to be always, he kept his thoughts captive.

"I asked you to stay because I wanted Jade to have a semblance of a normal life. But I also wanted to prove to you that I'd changed." She shoved her hands into her pock-

ets and averted her eyes. Sunlight sparkled on the trees.
Horses grazed in the pasture on her left, their coats shining with health. Shadow lifted her head from her small
paddock near the barn. Tenley had turned her out for a
few hours after their lesson, and they were supposed to
be on their way to train Rascal, but Mac's steps angled
them toward the fence instead of the house.

Jade raced out of the main house, Zeus and Rascal at
her heels.

Tenley's time alone with Mac dwindled with every step.
She had to get this out now, before she lost her nerve or
he cut her off. "I'm sorry. I'm sorry I wasn't at the church
for our wedding. And I'm sorry that I never told you why.
I was ashamed."

"We were supposed to be a team." Mac spun to face
her. "I told you everything. We promised never to keep
secrets from each other."

"I didn't want to hurt you." She folded her arms across
her stomach and hugged her elbows tight. "I was trying
to protect you."

He took a step back. They stopped walking and now
stood face-to-face. "From what? What was so bad that
you couldn't tell me?"

It was time to tell him everything. She knew that, but
her stomach clenched and her legs shook.

Jade ran toward them, and her approaching shouts carried on the wind.

Tenley had time for one confession. The one that
started her downward spiral. "Dad's accident was my
fault. I called and asked him to pick me up."

"Ten—"

The softness in his eyes and voice, the way he held out
a hand to her, threatened every wall she'd built to keep

them apart. All she had to do was tell him the rest, and he'd be gone from her life for good. And so would Jade. He'd never allow Jade to come back here once he knew the depth of Tenley's betrayal.

She took a step away from Mac, from the comfort he offered, and tightened her grip on her elbows to still her shaking hands. "I left before he could pick me up. Decided to go out with a few of our friends. When he couldn't find me, he drove around town. That's when another driver hit him." She shuddered her way through the confession. The accident should've woken her up to her toxic habits, but it only sent her spiraling deeper.

It wasn't until she spent her wedding day in the neighboring town's jail that she wizened up to the truth about herself and her future. There'd have been no keeping it quiet if Sheriff Hanks knew about Tenley's overnight visit.

The past was a gulf between them. No bridge or road could connect their hearts ever again. She'd only hurt him.

Jade skidded to a stop, her hair flying wild around her face. She shot a smile at them both. "Time to train?"

"Yep." Mac dropped his hand to his side. He let out a loud whistle, and Zeus came streaking across the yard.

The dog leaped over ditches and slid under fences until he reached Mac's side.

Jade's jaw dropped. "Whoa. That's so cool. Can Rascal learn how to do that?" She attempted to whistle and ended up spitting and spluttering.

Mac chuckled and ruffled her hair. "We'll teach him."

As though he knew they wanted him, the pup ambled along in Zeus's wake. His ears perked up straight, and he trotted over to Zeus before plopping onto the ground with a huff.

"Jade, if you think Zeus is impressive now, you should

see him and Mac work together." Tenley nodded at Mac, a sly smile emerging. She'd only seen them in videos that Amber recorded when Mac trained, but it was enough to raise chill bumps on her arms. "Why don't you show her?"

He held up both hands in defense. "That's not necessary."

"Oh, but I think it is." She cocked her head to the side, daring him. When he refused to relent, she wagged her head at him. "Come on. Please?" She pushed aside the heaviness of their earlier conversation and focused on adding a teasing tone to her voice. "I've never seen him work in real life. It's always fascinated me how Zeus understands your commands."

"Yeah, please, Uncle Mac." Jade danced around him, grabbed his hands, and pulled. "Please. Please. Pretty please."

He shot a glare at Tenley, but it didn't hold the usual venom. He almost seemed proud at the chance to show off. "Well, since Zeus might not be my partner for much longer, I suppose it won't hurt to have one last training session. Should keep him in shape in case the captain lets him stay on the force."

With that news hanging rent-free in her head, Tenley gaped at Mac. "Zeus is retiring?"

"What's retiring?" Jade asked.

"Nothing." Mac scrubbed his hands over his face. "Forget I said anything. It's not important." He took a step away from them and snapped his fingers in Zeus's direction. "You two stand by the fence, and I'll take Zeus through a few exercises."

Jade took Tenley's hand and led her to the split-rail fence. Tenley helped Jade climb onto the top rail and settled a hand on her knee to keep the girl steady.

Mac met Zeus's eyes. He made a hand motion, and Zeus trotted to Mac's side. Tenley tried to understand the movements that Mac made, but she lost track of them in the beauty of their partnership. Zeus settled by Mac's side and looked up. His gaze never wavered. It was as though they were connected through thought alone.

Mac strode across the field with Zeus planted firmly against his leg. Then the dog moved to stand between Mac's knees. With every step Mac took, the dog kept pace. Mac dropped to a crouch, and Zeus sank to his belly. When Mac stood and pointed, Zeus zipped off in a blur of legs.

Mac whistled, and Zeus whirled, coming back to rest in front of Mac. They were in sync, tuned into each other in a way Tenley had only seen with Callie and her mare, Glow. It was the kind of connection Tenley longed to have with Shadow. The mare wanted comfort from Tenley but little else. It was a small improvement in a long journey of overcoming the mare's fears.

Mac gave Zeus another signal, and the dog lay down on the ground and belly crawled forward a dozen feet. Mac crept to the dog's side and patted his back. When he held up a tennis ball, Zeus leaped to his feet and waited for Mac to throw it across the field.

Jade clapped wildly, almost pitching off the rail from her enthusiasm. Mac grinned and bowed at the waist. Tenley joined Jade in clapping loudly and let out a whistle.

Mac blushed beneath his cowboy hat, turning his cheeks rosy. Tenley's own face scrunched in a grin at the sight. She'd never expected him to be self-conscious of his work with Zeus or to dislike performing for them. She found it endearing for the always confident cowboy to have a flaw.

He trotted back to them and held out a hand.

Jade slapped her palm to his and scooted from the rail. "Show Rascal how to do that."

"We will. But he needs to learn a few basic commands first. Start with the small stuff. Let him gain some confidence before we ask him to do the big things. Even puppies need confidence if you want them to become well-adjusted dogs." Mac tweaked Jade's ponytail and her grin widened.

Huh. Tenley let that rumble around for a minute. It made sense. They did the same things with horses. She or Brody never asked a horse to carry a rider before they were comfortable with a saddle and bridle first. They wouldn't ask an untrained colt to go through the obstacle course. Confidence. That's what Shadow needed.

Mac spent the next half hour showing Jade ways to teach Rascal. He showed the puppy how to sit and stay, with Zeus helping. Every time Mac gave an order, Zeus completed it, then looked at Rascal like he was saying, "See? This is what you're supposed to do."

By the time they finished, Rascal had the sit command down pat but still lunged after Jade every time she tried to back away while he was in stay position.

Jade huffed and put her hands on her hips. "You're not listening."

"He'll get there." Mac's calm reassurance caused Jade's forlorn expression to clear.

She hopped through the thick grass like a rabbit. "Will you come to the fair?"

Mac's eyebrows winged upward. "The fair isn't until August."

"It's the end of the school year. Homecoming." Tenley plucked a blade of grass and rolled it between her fingers until it blurred. "They moved the date up a few years ago. August is too hot, so the city council decided to mix the school's field day with the homecoming and make a huge event over at the fairgrounds."

"Ah." Mac scratched the back of his neck and then rested his right hand on his hip. "I guess I could put in an appearance. For old times' sake."

"Yay!" Jade barreled into his legs, almost knocking him down.

Tenley stifled a laugh.

"Jade?" Luke shouted from across the pasture. He stood on his front porch, hands cupped around his eyes like binoculars.

Jade popped up from the grass and waved her hands overhead. "Can I go play with Luke?" She looked at Tenley first, then faced Mac.

Indecision warred on Mac's face, and Tenley let him take the lead. He needed to understand the full brunt of what he was taking on.

"Isn't your riding class about to start?"

Tenley checked her phone. "In an hour."

"So I can go?" Jade bounced from foot to foot. "I want to show Luke what Rascal can do." The pup leaped up at the sound of his name and raced around Jade's legs, yipping on every bounce.

Zeus yawned and stretched out for a nap.

Mac moved closer to Tenley, a question brewing in his eyes.

She twitched her shoulders, refusing to let him persuade her. This was his call.

Luke looked over his shoulder, nodded, then jumped off the porch and ran a few steps. "Mama says we can play in the backyard. Can you come?"

Jade settled into her pleading position, hands clasped under her chin and eyes wide as saucers.

"Yeah. Okay. Stay in the backyard with Luke until I come to get you for class." He huffed like one of the horses but softened when Jade squealed and threw her arms around his legs in a tight squeeze.

She shot over to Tenley next and repeated the move. "I can't wait to ride today. We're going to trot!" She bolted before Tenley could answer.

Mac's easy expression dropped into a glower.

Tenley held up a hand to stall him. "It's a trot, Mac. You've already seen her ride at a gallop. Freckles trots like a little old man. She's perfectly safe."

He seemed about to say something, but nothing emerged.

Tenley tightened her ponytail and turned on her heel. "I'm going to work with Shadow for a bit before class."

The last thing she expected was for Mac to fall into step beside her. He kept quiet until they reached the mare's pasture. Then he looped his arms over the rail and tipped his hat up. "Why did you rescue her?"

The question took her by surprise, and Tenley answered without really thinking it through. "Because I could. She needed me. No one else at that auction saw what I did."

"And what did you see?" He peered at her from under his hat brim, genuine curiosity burning in his eyes.

"I saw a horse that had never been given a chance. She was scared and skinny. She needed help that no one else wanted to give." Tenley gripped the wooden rail until splinters pierced her palms.

Mac continued staring, looking at her, through her, to something she couldn't fathom. "You saved her." He nodded, his assessment complete. "And the equine therapy? What's that about?"

"When Dad..." Tears clogged Tenley's throat, surprising her. She stopped and blinked rapidly, pushing back the onslaught of emotion. "After Dad's accident, I felt lost. Out of control. The only place I felt safe was in the barn with the horses."

"You never told me that." Mac's voice was quiet and without censure. He didn't blame her or ask for a reason, he simply stated the obvious.

Tenley held on tighter to the railing. "There were a lot of things I didn't tell you back then. I wish I had. Maybe things could've been different." She whispered the last almost too low for him to hear. The urge to ask for a second chance flared bright, but she stuffed it down where it belonged.

He'd gotten over her. Married Laura and had a life of his own in Chicago. There was no more Mac-and-Tenley and never would be again.

"Why didn't you come to the funeral?" The question popped out before she knew she planned on asking it.

Mac jolted back and hissed between his teeth. Zeus looked up from where he lay on Mac's boots. He gave the area a serious perusal, then lowered his head to the dirt. Tenley never even heard the dog approach or come to rest with Mac.

Mac took off his hat and settled it on the fence post. Sweat dampened his hair, curling it at the edges and plastering it across his forehead. It shouldn't look as good as it did. Tenley curled her fingers into the rail to keep from reaching over and brushing the hair back.

"A few days before the accident, my partner and I found ourselves in the middle of a sticky situation. We were on a call." He paused and pinched the bridge of his nose. "I broke protocol. I had a gut feeling that my partner was in danger, so I abandoned my post and ran after him. Shoved him to the ground when I thought I saw one of the guys pull a gun."

Tenley's heart lodged in her throat. She read the rest of the story in his expression, in the way he'd moved. His admission upon arrival that Zeus was injured. And moments ago when he said the dog might not return to active duty. "You were shot." She made it a statement, but he nodded to confirm.

She lifted a hand to her mouth, covering the shocked inhale and quelling the sudden urge to throw herself into his arms.

"How bad?" She spoke through her fingers, muffling the words.

Mac ran a hand along his ribs. "Lucky shot. Went under my vest and chipped my shoulder blade. Punctured a lung."

Words failed her. He spoke about getting shot like it happened every day. Like it didn't matter. "And your partner? He's okay?"

"He's fine. Zeus took the second bullet while protecting me. Cole got the guys." Mac grabbed his hat and jammed it onto his head. "You told me once that I had a savior complex. That saving people wasn't just what I did, but that I'd made it my identity." He nodded toward Shadow. "Maybe you were right. But maybe you have the same complex."

"I'm no one's savior." She laughed off the idea.

Mac faced her, eyes inscrutable. "No? Then, why did you open an equine therapy center? Why do you spend day after day saving kids from the pain wreaking havoc on their lives? Why did you save a horse that no one else wanted?"

"Because I know what it's like to be them." She shoved away from the fence. "I know what it's like to be drowning in grief and guilt and feel like there's no place to turn. I know what it's like to look at your family and have them stare back at you like you're a stranger. I know what it's like to think that if I'd only made a different choice, then my life would be better." The floodgates tore open, spewing her thoughts with every breath. "I forced you to walk away from me because I knew it was only a matter of time before I ruined you too. You were better off without me. You just couldn't see it."

She darted between the rails, cutting off Mac before he could reply.

And then she ran.

The same as always. Because she couldn't face seeing the truth once it came to Mac. She couldn't face knowing she'd almost lost him. Almost seven years in Chicago and he'd never been injured. Until now.

Tenley ran hard and fast down the packed dirt trail the horses had created through years of tromping across the field. It led her into the woods, where sunlight stopped and gloom ruled all.

"Does your dad know you blame yourself?" Mac's voice penetrated the woods.

She startled. She hadn't heard him following behind.

He approached from the side, hat askew and not the least bit out of breath.

He'd followed her. Because of course he would. This was Mac. He'd obviously not changed. Even now, when she pushed him away, he came back for more punishment. He eyed her, and his eyes flashed with what looked like concern. "You never told him. What about Brody and

Molly? Does anyone know you're carrying around all this unnecessary guilt?"

"Unnecessary?" She glared at him from her spot under an oak. Bark dug into her shoulder when she shifted, but she held her ground. "You want to talk about unnecessary? *You* blame me." She waved a hand at his incredulous expression. "Ever since you came back, *you've* been on my case. *You've* been hurtful and mean. Which in Mac speak, means you blame me. I get you despising me for jilting you. I do. I'd have a hard time forgiving someone for that. But acting like I'm going to hurt Jade? Making my classes sound like I'm practicing high-speed sporting events on horseback without any training? What's that about?"

She launched the diatribe at him, hoping and praying it would make him go away. Every word scored her heart and gouged at her peace of mind. It was the truth but spoken with a spite that she never felt toward Mac.

Mac put his back against an oak tree directly in front of her. He hooked his thumbs in his belt loops and crossed one ankle over the other. "Go on." He caught her gaze and held it. "The only way we're getting past this is to get it all out in the open."

"What if I don't want to get past it?" she asked.

"You're the one who begged me to stay in Tamarack Springs." He lifted a shoulder. "Co-guardianship, right?"

He was messing with her. He had to be. Sure, he'd said he'd think about it, but this wasn't merely thinking. This was actively asking for a possible solution. Her anger dried up as fear took over. "You're not moving back to Chicago?"

"I don't know." He rolled his shoulder and offered her a rueful smile. "Getting shot, spending days laid up in a hospital bed. Missing Amber's funeral and finding out about you and Jade. It all overwhelmed me, Ten. I've just been trying to survive. Every time I come up for air, there's something else there ready to push me back down."

She understood that. That feeling of drowning had chased her for years.

"When Laura died, I said that was it." He made a slashing motion through the air. "I wasn't going to love anyone else ever again. It hurt too much. I'd lost too much already."

A breeze slipped between them, fluttering Mac's sleeves and dragging Tenley's ponytail into the tree's bark. She lost her voice, her thoughts, her heart, as Mac revealed the hurt burrowed deep down inside. He'd always held things close. Sometimes she forgot just how good he was at burying his emotions. Now they were on full display.

"When I found out about Amber. About Jade. I lost it. I've been living on autopilot since then. Seeing you again, being here where all our memories collide, it's ripping me apart." He turned away from her. "I don't know if I can stay. Or if I can get past what happened between us. But I think I have to try. And if I'm going to try, then you do too. Starting with talking to your family about the accident."

He strode away, leaving her heart a twisted mess that might never beat right ever again. He'd always been able to do that, twist her up in knots and make her think.

And he was right. She had to confess to her family. She should've done it years ago.

And sometime soon, she'd have to tell *him* the rest.

Chapter Ten

A twinge of homesickness hit Mac when he pulled into the fairgrounds. People mingled, laughing and enjoying the bright May morning. It felt odd having this many people rushing around this early on a Saturday morning. But that was Tamarack Springs. An event like this was one of the highlights of the year, and the whole town turned out for it. School had ended and the whole town wanted to celebrate.

He'd managed to spend the last week going back and forth from Amber's house to the ranch with Jade without any more meltdowns.

They were making progress, and with school over, he could work toward a new routine.

He stepped out of his truck and released Zeus. The dog stayed glued to Mac's leg even with the leash attached to his brand-new collar. No vest today. Mac patted the dog's ribs. "Enjoy yourself. This may be the only time you ever get to see this." He expected a phone call from his captain any day. No matter whether Zeus went back to work or not, he hoped he'd get to keep the dog once he went into retirement. The department would put him into a conditioning program centered around conditioning police canines into becoming family pets.

"Mac." Sheriff Hanks waved from a blue-roofed tent tucked in the corner of the fairway.

Mac made his way over, people giving way to him and Zeus with barely a glance.

"Good to see you." Sheriff Hanks pumped Mac's hand, then gestured over his shoulder. "You remember Bricker and Smith."

Mac grinned at the two deputies he'd worked alongside while training for a position as one of Tamarack's own deputies. Before...well, before he and Tenley fell apart. "Good to see you both." He shook their hands and motioned at the crowd. "Quite a turnout today."

"Just wait." Bricker took off his black baseball cap and wiped sweat from his hairline. He resettled the cap and rested a hand on his hip.

Mac took note of the positioning. Bricker's hand grazed the grip of his firearm in a relaxed manner.

It was the same move Mac found himself making time and again. He'd left his gun behind until his administrative leave ended. If it ended. Even after a month off duty, he kept reaching for that assurance. It felt wrong to have his trust in a weapon. A weapon hadn't saved his life when he shoved his partner out of the way.

"Got a minute?" Sheriff Hanks's question tugged Mac away from his thoughts.

He nodded. "Sure."

Hanks jerked his head toward the back of the tent, where traffic was less congested. "You boys man the table."

Bricker snorted and crossed muscular arms. He nudged Smith with an elbow. "You remember that time Mac hit back-to-back home runs?"

Smith whistled. "Now, that was a sight." He winced and shook his head. "Sure wish we had someone like him on the team today. We'd beat those Bridgeport city cops without a lick of trouble."

"You need another man?" Mac played into their game, letting them feel like they were in charge. It was an old ploy. One they'd used when he was a wet-behind-the-ears greenie who didn't know a thing about being a deputy but knew he wanted to help people. He lifted his shoulders in a casual shrug. "Haven't played in a few years. Might be rusty."

Smith and Bricker eyed each other. Bricker gave way first, his grin crawling out until it forced his eyes closed. "Six o'clock. Don't be late."

Mac tapped the brim of his cowboy hat and followed Hanks to the open area behind the tent.

"Glad to see all of you getting along." Hanks palmed his chin. He looked everywhere and nowhere, his posture appearing nonthreatening. Mac knew it was a ruse. The man could strike out in any direction at a moment's notice. "Been meaning to talk to you again. Never seemed like a good time. Probably no better now, but this has been weighing on me something fierce, and it's time I get it off my chest."

"I'm all ears, Sheriff."

"I mentioned it before and you shut me down pretty hard." Sheriff Hanks tilted his head to the side and scrutinized Mac from head to toe. "I was serious about that job offer. Stick around and come back to work for me."

Mac's mouth dropped open. Zeus pressed his head into Mac's hand, and he snapped his teeth closed.

Hanks watched through narrowed eyes. "I don't know your situation in Chicago. Maybe you're happy there. Maybe you're not. But if you're looking to come home, the position is yours."

"Sheriff." Mac thumbed the spot where his gun would be if he wore his uniform. The missing weight tugged on him. "I'm a mess. I can't say if I'm coming or going." A yearning hit him with a full-on body blow. A need to stay here where he knew the people walking down the street. A place where people greeted each other with smiles.

Was this the answer he'd been praying for?

"What about Zeus?" He motioned at the dog sitting on his foot. "I don't know what's going to happen with him. My captain is considering retiring him."

Sheriff Hanks eyed Zeus and then the fairgrounds that were steadily growing busier. "That's up to you. Adopt him and bring him with you. If he's capable, we'll consider adding him to the force with you. Maybe he's not up for running down drug dealers, but he'd be handy for sniffing out Bricker's candy stash." The sheriff rubbed his palms together and wiggled his eyebrows. "Hunt down rogue hamburgers at Granny's."

That easy?

Mac gave in and grinned. "I'll think about it." The simple phrase had become his mantra since returning to Tamarack. Everything he'd ever wanted out of life was still here, in the only place he'd ever called home. "I need to find Jade." The arena sat atop the hill, beckoning him closer.

Tenley would be there, along with Brody, Callie and Jade. His pulse ratcheted up at the thought of seeing Tenley again. Ever since she told him about how she blamed herself, she never strayed far from his thoughts. What else had she hidden from him? They'd always said no secrets. He'd meant it, and from his side, he could say that he'd never kept anything from her. But now he wondered just how much of their relationship had been real. The last thing he'd expected was for Tenley to withhold information from him. Especially something as big as blaming herself for her father's accident, which happened four years before their disastrous almost-wedding.

Four years that turned into a little over a decade. How much strength had it taken to carry that burden alone?

It was time he stopped hiding from the truth in his past. Tenley had offered to explain why she'd jilted him at the altar. He hadn't really wanted to know. Out of desperation or some sense of self-preservation, he'd asked her not to tell him.

No more. No more hiding. Time to clear the air and see where their lives might go from here.

Funnel cakes and apple pie. Two of Tenley's favorite smells. Now that she was here, she didn't mind Brody roping her into helping with the pony rides. Tamarack Springs's annual end-of-the-school-year and homecoming fair was not to be missed. The only thing weighing on her today was knowing whether Mac planned on staying. They hadn't spoken since the confrontation in the woods. Mac kept his distance while still showing up for Jade's classes. The space felt unnatural, but Tenley appreciated the way it helped ease the tug-of-war in her heart every time he was there.

They could do this, coexist and still take care of Jade. There were no rules or laws that said they should revisit the idea of being a couple. They could raise Jade into a healthy adult this way. She believed that, even if the idea of more with Mac left her gazing up at the mountains long after night fell as dreams of a different future played out.

But it wasn't meant to be. She'd thought maybe they had a chance. Mac insinuated as much. Getting past what happened was one thing. Having a second chance with Mac was another, and it was completely out of the question.

Someone shouted her name, drawing Tenley's attention back to the present.

The fairgrounds burst with every color of the rainbow. All along the edge, colorful canopies kept the sun from frying people as they sold their wares. Everything from hand-sewn quilts to books, even a booth filled with cookware, covered the grassy embankment. Patrons took advantage of what little shade they could find, fanning their faces and enjoying glasses of cold iced tea or lemonade.

Food vendors lined the opposite side, Molly smack in the middle. Luke ran around the table. A smear of icing along his cheek spoke all too clearly of eager energy. His teacher approached Molly and made several hand motions. Molly nodded and Luke took his teacher's hand before they skipped over to the bounce castle.

Anything a person could dream of could be found here. Even deep-fried Oreos. Her stomach rumbled at the scent, and she headed toward Patrick's food truck. He'd painted it since last year and added Brewsters in fancy block type. Tenley stood on tiptoes to peer over the people in front of her.

Patrick greeted each customer by name, the same as he did in his coffee shop, located beside Granny's. He caught Tenley's eye, and his smile broadened. "How's my favorite Jacobs doing today?"

"Fine and dandy." She took a step closer as the line inched forward. "Off to find that brooding brother of mine."

"He'd better get over that." Patrick gave an exaggerated eye roll. "I might have something that'll sweeten his disposition." Patrick disappeared from the truck's window, and a woman took his place.

By the time Tenley made it to the front of the line, Patrick returned with a cup carrier loaded down with four drinks and a stack of donuts. "There you go. No charge."

"Nope." Tenley waved her money. "I can pay."

"Never said you couldn't. Consider this a thank-you for those lessons you've been giving my nephew. Never seen him happier than he is after his Saturday ride." Patrick pushed the carrier closer. "Take it. I won't hear otherwise."

Tenley stuffed the money into her pocket. "I'll get it back to you somehow."

He chuckled. "I don't doubt it. But not today. Today, it's my treat."

Tenley hefted the drink carrier and stepped out of line. She spun the cups around, looking for her own, when Mac's name in a heavy scrawl stopped her in her tracks. That sneaky man. She bit the inside of her cheek and resumed her trek up the gravel drive leading to the arena, where Brody and Callie would soon arrive.

She worked her way through the crowd, nodding hello to those she knew and stopping to talk when someone waved her over.

Winding her way around a cluster of kids waiting in line for a train-shaped bounce castle, someone shouted her name. Tenley was surprised she heard them amid the children's clamor and the general noise created by half of the town crammed together on the same five acres. Turning toward the sound, Mac waved at her from under the Tamarack Springs Sheriff Department's tent. Seeing him there in his casual clothes amid a slew of blue uniforms ignited something in her midsection.

Mac never caused butterflies. No. The feeling he

evoked felt more like a herd of buffalo stampeding across the plain.

Apprehension tickled her spine. The emotions he set loose said that being with him could be detrimental to her emotional boundaries. Her sobriety took all her effort. Adding a rekindled relationship with the man whose heart she stomped broke all the rules.

He ran to her.

The buffalo in her gut stampeded again. Mercy but the man looked good.

"Where are you headed?" He nudged his hat up and peered at her from under the brim. "Can we talk?"

"I'm on my way to help with the pony rides." She lifted the drinks in the direction of the arena and didn't bother hiding her annoyance at his sudden appearance. "Patrick sent this for you." She turned the cup carrier where his drink faced him.

Mac grinned and took the cup. "Good man, that Patrick. I was in need of a caffeine boost." He took a slow sip. "Need help with the horses?"

No. Sweat trickled down her spine. "I can manage."

"Which means you don't want me to help, not that you don't need help." He fell in step beside her, aiming them at the gate.

Brody had the trailer backed in and the gate down. He and Callie led the horses out, one by one, while Jade watched from outside the fence.

Tenley resisted an eye roll in Mac's direction. "I can't stop you."

"Good." Mac's smile appeared genuine. It faltered after a few seconds. "I'm playing baseball tonight with the Sheriff's team. Can you stay? We'll talk afterward."

Stay and watch him play like old times? It might be her

last chance to see him as the Mac she knew and remembered fondly. Not the hardened version he'd showboated around earlier. The one she barely recognized. Maybe the old Mac was making a comeback.

"Sure. I'll stay. I'll bring Jade so she can see her uncle hit another double home run." She smiled when he ducked his head.

"Been a long time since I played. Not sure I have another double in me."

She squeezed his forearm before ducking between the rails. "I believe in you." She hurried toward Brody and Callie. "Hey, hold up."

"Is this a stick-up?" Brody's smile creased his cheeks.

Callie's laugh caught Tenley by surprise, and when Brody joined in, Tenley grinned and held up the drink carrier. "I was going to give you these. Patrick made them special for you." She turned away. "But if you're going to crack jokes, then I'll drink them myself."

Brody cut in front of her, blocking her exit with his body and horse. "Oh no. You're not getting away with my coffee." He grabbed the cup and lifted it to his nose. After a deep inhale, he frowned at Tenley. "You didn't put salt in it, did you?"

"First of all, that was an accident." Tenley held up one finger, then another. "Second, would I really sabotage a Brewsters coffee?"

"Yes." Callie and Brody said simultaneously.

Tenley chuckled at their gaping expressions. "Yeah. Okay. I would. But I didn't." She reached for Brody's cup. "You want me to take a sip and prove it to you?"

"No thanks." Brody tucked the cup close to his chest and thrust the lead rope at her. "Can you take Pepper over to the rail with Spirit? I'll get the next one unloaded."

She took the lead and nodded once. "You got it, boss." Their laughter followed her as she turned and walked the horse to the white rail.

A line of kids formed behind Jade as they approached the horses, reminding Tenley of ducklings. She wiggled her eyebrows at Mac, doing her best to remove the strain from earlier.

Jade climbed onto the rail beside Spirit's head, stroking the gelding's mane.

Tenley hopped up beside her. "Hey, you. How was the ride over with Brody and Callie?"

"Great." Jade beamed. "He let me watch the horses on his camera."

"Sounds fun." Mac stepped in. "He mentioned last week that he wanted cameras installed in the trailers. I didn't expect him to get it done this fast."

"That's Brody. He's never one to sit still." Tenley chuckled and slid back to the ground. She checked over the horses. Once they were all geared up and settled in a line, Tenley motioned for Jade to hop into Pepper's saddle. "Mac, you have Jade. I'll grab the next one. Two laps around the arena, then switch."

He tapped the brim of his hat with one finger in his version of a cowboy salute. It warmed Tenley to see him slowly breaking through that wall and coming back into the Mac she knew…and loved?

She forced a smile into place and untied Spirit while motioning for the little girl next in line to come up. "Hi, I'm Tenley. What's your name?"

"Becky." The girl bobbed her pigtails and smiled, showing a gap where her front teeth should have been.

"Well, Becky, would you like to go for a ride?"

Another nod.

Brody and Callie each took a horse and formed a line behind Tenley and Spirit.

Tension melted away under the kids' scrutiny. Tenley adjusted the mounting block and rested her hand on Spirit's neck. "Step right up there and into the saddle." A couple stood by the rail, faces wreathed in anxiety. "Mom. Dad. Do you want to walk with her?"

Relieved breaths expelled and smiles took over.

Motioning them forward, Tenley gave gentle directions. "Why don't you each take a side? You can rest your hands on the saddle if you like. And let's walk on."

Spirit took a step, and the woman gasped. Becky laughed, the sound bright as the sunlight. "I'm riding. Look. I'm riding."

"You sure are." Becky's dad spoke up while her mom remained tight-lipped.

Mac winked at Tenley across the arena, sending a blush soaring into her cheeks. How did he do that? Why, after all these years, did he still affect her this way? She turned her attention to Becky. The girl struck up an animated conversation, telling all she knew about horses. This one had the horse bug, reminding Tenley of herself at that age. She'd never outgrown it. Unlikely Becky would either.

After two rounds of the arena, Tenley helped Becky dismount and nodded at her parents. "I would apologize, but I think it's too late."

The dad chuckled. "Pretty sure I see a horse in our future."

While the mom frowned, Becky squealed and pirouetted.

"My brother trains horses. Brody Jacobs. If you decide to buy, look him up." She slid a card toward the man, who took it with a smile.

* * *

Three hours of walking kids around the ring in the sweltering heat and Mac was ready to dive headfirst into an ice bath. Or a river. Whichever he found first.

Maybe then he'd be in the mood to play baseball. Right now, the idea of any activity other than sitting with a cool drink in his hand felt like torture.

Zeus lifted his head from where he'd been napping in the shade and yawned. He'd been patient all morning. Mac had let a few of the kids pet him but kept an eye on Zeus to ensure the dog didn't mind the attention. *He didn't*, Mac thought with a laugh.

Brody and Callie had stayed with them for the first two hours. Once the line slowed, Tenley had told them to go enjoy themselves. They'd taken Jade with them so she could enjoy time with her friends. Tenley had tried to drive Mac off too, saying she could handle it herself.

Despite the heat, he found himself enjoying chatting with the kids and walking them around the arena. Their awe and delight brightened his day. It reminded him of years gone by. He'd grown up riding horses with Tenley and the others. The sense of awe had become normal at some point, and he wanted that back.

"I need food." He tied Snickers—a pale brown horse with a single spot on his rump and a salt-and-pepper mane and tail—in the shade beside a pail of fresh water, and for half a second considered dunking his head in the five-gallon bucket.

"You always need food." Tenley rolled her eyes. Sweat glistened on her neck and arms and dampened the dark hair framing her face. She'd pulled it back earlier, but tiny wisps escaped and stuck to her cheeks.

He itched to brush them away. Mac patted his stomach and groused. "I'm a growing boy."

Tenley gave him a slow perusal, her eyes lingering over his shoulders. With a shake of her head, she started removing Spirit's saddle. The gelding pushed his nose into the water bucket and swirled it around, sending a waterfall onto Tenley's calves. "Nice." She shook out one foot.

"They'll dry in no time out here." Mac took off his hat and wiped a trail of sweat from his face. "I'm turning into a raisin. Or a dry husk of corn."

"Stop complaining." Tenley threw a rag at him. "You sound worse than a toddler who's lost his binky."

"What's a binky?" He rubbed the rag over Snickers' coat, drying sweat while the horse groaned, cocked a hind hoof and relaxed.

Tenley lifted Spirit's head and wiped a clean rag over the sweat-dampened hide. "A pacifier. Have you never been around babies?"

Except for the few times he'd attended a birthday party for one of his partner's kids, or when Amber brought Jade to visit, no. Mac leaned into the work, hoping his extra effort covered the sudden discomfort. "Work in Chicago is different than here. Not much time for kids. By the time I got to people, it was usually too late." He clamped his teeth before he set loose more words.

"I'm sorry." The somberness of Tenley's tone brought his head up. She couldn't understand, not really, but the way she looked at him, with sadness and empathy in her eyes, she showed sincerity.

Snickers nudged Mac's pocket, a soft whicker shivering through the horse's body. No doubt he wanted a treat after all his hard work. Mac fished one from his jeans and let the horse lip it from his palm.

She kept her back to him, but her movements lacked her usual smooth grace.

"How about a trip to the dunking booth?" Mac tossed the dirty rag into the grooming box and dusted off his hands. "I could use a cooling off."

"Let me call Molly. She wanted to drive the horses home. The last text she sent said she'd already sold out of all her baked goods. She left the tent up so people could come by and talk, but I think she's about reached her limit of socialization for today." Talking about her sister put the light back in her eyes.

Mac tracked her movements as she paced up and down in front of the stands, phone to her ear. Doubt niggled the back of his mind.

Coming to his side, Tenley rubbed her hand over Snickers' mane. "It's all set. Molly and Luke will take the horses home, but she'll come back for me when I'm ready to go."

"There's no sense in that. I'll drive you home. You said you're staying for the game." He narrowed his eyes when she protested. "Let Molly enjoy her night. I'll drop you and Jade off."

"Only if you let me pay for your dinner."

Unnecessary…but Mac took a long look at Tenley, from her fidgeting hands to her toes tapping in time with the band on stage at the bottom of the hill off to the right. "Fine. If you can dunk me, you can pay for dinner."

"Deal." Glee emanated from Tenley, drawing light to her eyes. Sweaty, dirty and tired, she still looked beautiful to him.

They loaded up the horses and waited for Molly and Luke to climb into the truck and pull away. Then he grabbed Zeus's leash and they left the arena.

They weaved through the crowd, the shouts and shrieks

coming from every direction. Passing a blue tent, the smell of funnel cakes caused Mac's mouth to water. Tenley shook her head. "Not yet. There's a water tank with your name on it."

He let her lead him away, his stomach grumbling a complaint.

A soggy man pulled himself from the tank as they approached.

"Hey, I'll take the next one if you don't care." Mac held Zeus's leash out to Tenley.

She took it from him and moved away.

The man slapped Mac on the shoulder. "Water's cold. Have fun."

"Yeah, Ten, have fun." Mac sent her a grin while he removed his shoes and climbed the four ladder rungs and settled onto the narrow platform. Dropping his feet into the lukewarm water, Mac waited. A line, several kids deep, cheered when Mac waved.

The first kid he remembered seeing around town. Travis, senior in high school. Deputy Smith's oldest kid. Travis hurled the sandbag, nicking the circle's edge. He groaned.

Mac slapped his knees. "Come on, Travis. You can do better than that."

Travis squinted at the target and wound up for the pitch, sandbag tight in his palm. He released, the bag slamming into the red paddle and sending Mac into the water.

He came up with a smile. In this heat, he welcomed any form of liquid.

Tenley smirked from her place in line, her smile widening each time a kid sent him under. Reaching the front of the line, she picked up a sandbag and tossed it up and down in her palm. "Having fun, Mac?"

"Absolutely. Give it your best shot."

She squeezed the bag and eyed him from the side. "Remember you said that." Her eyes brightened, and before Mac could reply, Tenley launched. The bag slapped the bullseye.

He fell with a plop and a splash and came up spluttering.

Tenley laughed and handed a bag to the next kid in line. "You forget, I don't like losing. Dinner's on me." Zeus gave Tenley an adoring look and followed her as she walked toward the funnel-cake truck.

He'd missed this. The easy camaraderie felt familiar yet brand-new.

Chapter Eleven

Tenley settled on the wooden bench closest to the dugout and shaded her eyes with her hand. Jade sat beside her, clapping and cheering. A ring of blue circled her mouth from the cotton candy Tenley bought on their walk to the baseball diamond.

Mac's long strides ate up the ground as he crossed to the dugout with Zeus at his side. Deputy Darren Smith pulled Mac into a hug, the two men talking and gesturing wildly like no time had passed.

Annoyance bit deep. Why did Mac get the homecoming of a lifetime while she was ignored? Except for the side glances shot her way, like now, from a mom and dad huddled around their two children as though Tenley's past could rub off on them.

Sure, she'd been a bit chaotic as a teenager, some of those times spent with the people who now gave her the side eye. They'd grown up, and so had she. Couldn't they see she'd changed?

Or maybe that was her insecurities rearing their ugly heads. Turning away, Tenley ignored them.

Mac picked up two bats, swinging them in easy arcs. Darren popped up at his side with a helmet in his hand. Mac swung, and Darren ducked. "Whoa, Mac. Take it easy. Save your energy for the game. I'd like to keep my face where it is."

"Sorry." Mac took a step back and dropped one bat. He gestured over his shoulder.

Darren caught Tenley's eyes. He nodded and Mac jogged her way. The opposing team filed onto the field.

"You still keep up with the games?" Mac curled his fingers into the fence, his hair—still damp from the dunk tank—curled under the cap he'd taken from his truck. "I could use your help if you do."

Her thoughts scattered. Put her up against a twelve-hundred-pound horse and she never batted an eye, but ten feet from Mac and a simple question and all coherent thought fled.

She shook off the feelings and met him at the fence, placing her fingers over his. "See the guy with the yellow cap? Watch out for him. He's got the best swing on the team." Tenley let the familiar smells of sweat and dirt rewind the years. She used to attend every one of Mac's games.

"Thanks for the warning."

Her breath caught, stomach churning as past and present collided. "Play your best game. No regrets. Leave it all on the field."

The smile he gave her—the sweet, innocent grin that had once told her how much he loved her—threatened to be her undoing as it rattled the cage where she kept memories of him locked away.

He slipped a finger out and hooked it around her thumb, but he didn't say the words to complete the ritual. *As long as I have you, there are no regrets.* That's what he was supposed to say. The lack of them hovered, as solid as a jail cell. The cage stopped rattling. Memories of what they'd been would never compare to the hurt. It didn't ease it and couldn't take it away.

Tenley nestled that core of pain against the traitorous beat of her heart that still yearned for Mac. For what was and could never be again.

What looked like regret flickered in his eyes before he turned and walked away.

Tamarack Springs' team, the Rangers, had a man on second and another on third, with two outs before Mac came up to bat. He stepped up to the plate and nearly took a pitch to the head. The umpire shouted, "Ball," and Mac readied for the next pitch. With runners on second and third, Mac settled in, his concentration on the pitcher.

Tenley chewed a fingernail, tension curling through her, as the pitcher wound up and released a fastball.

Mac connected, the crack of bat on ball sending Tenley to her feet with a shout. The ball sailed toward the outfield. Mac raced toward first. His foot slapped the base seconds before his teammate raced over home plate.

He hit second, while Darren raced home. The other team had the ball, winding it toward Mac as he lowered his head and barreled toward third.

Tenley jumped up and down, arms waving. "Slide, Mac!"

Jade joined her, screaming and jumping on the bench.

He glanced back and picked up speed before throwing himself into a slide that carried him safely to third base. Jumping to his feet, he whipped off his cap and waved it at the crowd as the stamping and shouting increased.

She clapped and cheered along with everyone else, the years falling away and taking her back, despite her attempts to stay. It was after one of Mac's games that Tenley had first tried alcohol. A little in the beginning, then more, until it overshadowed everything else in her life.

And after this game, she'd tell Mac all of it. The confession was a long time coming.

The next batter struck out, and Mac jogged off the field. He grabbed his glove and took up the shortstop position. His favorite. Not everyone could handle the intensity. He'd once told Tenley that he loved the constant action, knowing that other people depended on him. A hero complex in the making.

Her mind whirled with questions. Evidence of his heroism leaked out with everything he did. Protecting Jade. Saving his partner. Where did she fall in his circle of protection? Did she want to be there?

The man that Tenley had warned him about stepped up to the plate. Mac pounded his fist into his glove while shooting a look at Tenley. He rocked his weight left to right, ready to move in any direction. She'd seen him in action too many times to doubt his ability.

Darren let loose from the pitcher's mound. The batter swung and missed, a disgusted expression on his face. He pointed his bat at Darren, who threw his head back and laughed.

"Coming for you, Smith." The batter taunted.

Darren rolled his head from side to side. "Give it your best shot."

These matches were all fun and games. Though the competition and rivalry excited the crowd, they were all friends joined in the same cause. This year's fundraiser went to the Tamarack Springs Fire Department.

The teams were made up of police, firemen, EMTs and volunteers until they wrangled enough people for four baseball games. While the homecoming along the square boasted an arcade, bounce castles, food, music and games, known four counties wide, the real attraction came from the baseball diamond.

Sweat trickled down Tenley's back. She rolled her shoulders to ease the tickling sensation and sipped from her water bottle.

Jade grabbed her pink tumbler from the bench and gulped, then dragged the back of her wrist over her mouth. A streak of blue smeared her hand.

Mac swiped his face on his shoulder, leaving dirt and sweat on the white uniform.

Darren released another pitch. The batter connected, and the ball hurtled toward Mac.

His glove snapped in front of Mac's stomach, the slap of the ball meeting leather sending Tenley's heart into her throat.

Mac's face didn't change, but she knew what catching that ball cost him. The speed and power behind the swing, coupled with the smack and Mac's single step back with the glove pressed against his stomach, told her more than he'd ever admit. The impact had hurt him. But it wasn't in Mac to show his pain. Or to quit.

Like the time he'd broken his hand in football practice and not told the coach. He couldn't stand the idea of letting his team down and had played through the pain. They'd won that night and Mac had run off the field. Straight for her.

She needed to stop these trips down memory lane. No more ball games. She had to quit pretending things between them could go back to the way they were. She thought she'd managed, but being here, watching him, it brought it all back. She had to let him go.

Until she could look at him without so many mixed

emotions, it would be better for them both if she backed off. She couldn't put Jade at risk. Which is what would happen if Tenley gave in to the love hurtling around inside and begged Mac for a second chance. She'd keep to the plan and tell Mac everything tonight. Then she'd have no choice but to let him go.

Mac tightened his grip on the wheel, wincing when his palm reminded him how long it'd been since he caught that many hurtling baseballs. They'd won the game, putting him on cloud nine until he walked off the field and been unable to find Tenley and Jade. He finally checked his phone and found a text message that she'd be waiting for him at the truck.

Tenley hadn't spoken a word since her shout for him to slide during the first inning. Her aloof posture and closed-off expression pulled at his heartstrings.

They'd had such a good day together.

She punched buttons on his radio, brow furrowed, until she landed on an oldies rock station. Not good. Tenley only listened to oldies when she wanted to forget. It was funny the things he remembered about her. Little quirks of personality that he'd figured out over the years.

Like the fact that she owned enough Converse shoes to fill a closet but rarely wore them. When she did, the color she chose made a statement about how she felt that day.

Red when she wanted to be brave.

Purple when she was hurting.

Yellow when she was excited for a new adventure.

And oldies on the radio when she felt sad.

Leaning back with her hands pressed together between her knees, she stared out the window. Her reflection bounced back at him under the streetlights. Jade tucked her head against the back seat and closed her eyes. They'd discussed dinner, and since Tenley demanded he uphold their bargain that she owed him a meal, they'd settled on eating at her house. Then talk after Jade fell asleep. Nervous tension gripped him, and his left foot bounced against the floor.

He kept his eyes on the road but glanced occasionally at Tenley. "You okay?"

She lifted one shoulder, her expression aloof. "Fine."

Liar. "Music says different." He sent her a smile, but she refused to look his way.

"So, change it." The acidic barb hooked deep, no doubt as it was meant to. He never messed with her music. He knew how much she needed the relief that came from finding the right beat to express her mood.

This one was angry, yet somehow also sad. They rode without speaking, empty streets flashing by, child sleeping silently, until the road changed from country town to country road and trees encroached on the edges of the roadway.

Mac bumped down the drive and hooked a right toward the little cabin where Tenley lived with Jade. He put the truck in Park, and she slid from the seat. She opened Jade's door and scooped her up before Mac could protest.

Zeus whined from his spot beside her.

Tenley marched toward the house while Mac released Zeus.

Let her go or confront her? Confront was too strong. They'd agreed to talk, and if she was as nervous as him, it was no wonder she stomped away. Following her up the steps, the fine hairs on the back of his neck stood at attention. A seam of light highlighted her open front door.

He reached for Tenley to stop her, his arm going around her waist.

"Mac, wha—"

"Shh." He stuck a finger to his lips and dipped his head close to her ear. "Did you leave your front door open when you left this morning?"

Her eyes widened.

Good enough answer. With his arm still around her waist, he hauled her backward, one slow step at a time, until they reached his truck. Could someone have broken in? "Stay here." He motioned for Zeus, and they started forward.

"I probably didn't pull it closed all the way," Tenley hissed behind him.

Mac kept his focus on the door. "I'm not letting you take that chance." Not with Jade, and not with herself. *Lord, please help me keep them safe.* His throat convulsed on a tight swallow. This time when he prayed, it wasn't lip service. He'd stopped trusting God to protect him and those he loved. Maybe it was time for that to change.

Where had unbelief gotten him?

His shoulders knotted with tension. Would he be able to protect Jade? If only he knew where the threat would come from first. Tenley? Or something else?

He approached the house with Zeus at his side. His fingers inched toward his belt before he remembered he didn't have his gun. Probably for the best. "You and me, big guy." He patted Zeus and sent the dog inside.

They cleared the house room by room. Zeus never alerted to danger, and Mac didn't find anything out of place. Still, his nerves jangled and the space in his heart where Tenley lived ached.

When Mac stepped back onto the porch and motioned

for Tenley, she ran straight for him and gave him a swift punch to the arm—but it wasn't the angry kind. She held Jade on one hip and gripped the back of his shirt as she followed it with a hug. "Don't ever scare me like that again."

"I wasn't worried about me. I had Zeus." He played it off as nothing more than an exercise.

Tenley didn't buy it. She leaned back and glared at him. "You might not care what happens to you, but I do." She poked his shoulder for added emphasis.

"Can I go to bed now?" Jade yawned and scrubbed her hands over her eyes before lowering her head to Tenley's shoulder.

Tenley's eyes flashed to him. She took in a shuddering breath and seemed to search for words. "You want to tuck her in? I'll fix us something to eat. She ate during the ball game, so she should sleep all night."

Mac carefully took Jade and walked ahead of Tenley into the house. They parted ways in the living room, and by the time Mac tucked Jade in and returned, Tenley had steaks sizzling in a pan.

She frowned, and her shoulders bowed forward. Her body language screamed her weariness.

"These are almost done." A grin flashed. "How many stories did you read her?"

"Two." Mac sat in a kitchen chair and propped his head on his clenched fist with his elbow on the table. "Do you want me to help?"

"I'm good here." She flipped the steaks. "You can grab us some plates."

He stood and made his way over to the cabinets. They fell into an easy rhythm, one they'd developed over time and fell back into without hesitation. Tenley slid the steaks onto matching plates and spooned carrots alongside while

Mac grabbed the rolls from the oven and dropped them into a basket.

They moved to the table and sat across from each other. Tenley bowed her head, and her lips moved in a silent prayer. Mac gripped the plate and tried not to let the nervous energy send him reeling backward.

"Do you want to eat first, or talk?" Tenley slid her napkin into her lap and watched him beneath lowered lashes.

He felt her gaze, every second of it tightening the coil in his gut. "I don't think I can eat." Shameful as it was to let the steaks go to waste, he nudged his plate away.

Tenley did the same. "You can take it with you. If you want." She'd removed her hat before cooking, and now her hair curled around her face. She ran her hands over her head, laced her fingers together behind her neck and leaned back. It was meant to be a casual stance, but the harsh lighting cutting across her cheekbones and the way her arms trembled gave her away.

"Just tell me, Tenley." He leaned forward. "Tell me why."

"I wish it was that easy." She sighed and slipped a hand into her pocket. A coin glinted in her hand, and she gripped it in a tight fist before placing the coin on the table and pushing it toward him.

Mac picked it up. A gold tree of life stretched bare branches across the top of the coin. A purple six glinted in the center of the tree's trunk. Underneath the tree was the inscription To Thine Own Self Be True. "What's this?"

"There's no easy place to start." Tenley retracted her hand and tucked it into her lap. "I'm an alcoholic, Mac."

He reeled back as a hundred thoughts crashed in on him at once. Denial hit the forefront, and he shook his head. "No, you're not."

"Yes. I am. I'm sober. That's my six-year coin. I'll get

my seventh-year token soon. On what would've been our seven-year anniversary."

The implications hit him harder than a thousand baseballs to the stomach at once. His heartbeat stuttered and his vision wavered. He pulled in a deep breath to clear the black spots dancing before his eyes. How…how had he not known?

"Why?" He choked on the question.

Tenley's brow furrowed. She dug in, her face falling into an expression he didn't recognize. Anger? Fear? It combined into a new version of Tenley.

"I started drinking in high school. Didn't take me long to become addicted. When Dad had his accident, I tried to stop. The accident really was my fault. I was going to try to go home that night, but I didn't…" She shook her head and lowered her eyes to the table. "It gets worse," she said under her breath. "I went drinking the night before our wedding. Got arrested in Bridgeport. That's…" She started to cry. "That's why I missed our wedding."

The words were clipped and short. They said everything with succinct power and no frills. Words had become weapons, and these tore him apart.

"And after? You never called. Refused to talk to me. Your family turned me away for three days straight before…" His leg bounced up and down.

Tenley pulled her left leg under her and crossed her arms over her stomach. She twisted the hem of her shirt around her forefinger, her nervous tell from years ago. "I begged them not to tell you. I left for rehab on the day you showed up here. No phone and no visitors the first week."

"So you were here that day, and you didn't talk to me?" He leaned forward and put his head in his hands. "Brody and I argued in the barn. I knew he was holding back, but nothing I said convinced him to tell me where you were."

There was more to it than she was admitting. Mac knew that, yet he couldn't bring himself to ask the questions. Betrayal sucker punched him and sent him clambering to his feet. "You never told me." He paced, hands going up in the air. "You drank for four years and never said a word? How did I not know? I knew you," he said loudly. "I thought I knew you," his voice quiet.

She shook her head, shame twisting her features. "You didn't need my problems weighing you down." Her voice was quiet, but he heard the intensity in the words. The excuses.

He pointed a finger at her, and even though it shook, his voice remained even. "We promised each other forever. Marriage meant in sickness and in health. I was willing to make that commitment."

"You were willing because you didn't know what a mess I was." Tenley stood but didn't approach. "I never told you because it wasn't your problem to solve—and I was ashamed."

"I would've helped." He pressed his palms into the sides of his head, trying desperately to relieve the pressure building inside him.

"You would've tried to fix it." Tenley's tortured gaze met his. "Love means letting go when you know you're going to destroy. I was on a path that would've taken you down with me."

"That's ridiculous." He scoffed, but a thread of truth lingered in the back of his mind.

Tenley continued like he'd not spoke at all. "You were a brand-new deputy in the smallest town around. I was on the brink of a major disaster. If we'd gotten married, only God knows how long it would've taken before I fell hard enough to go to rehab."

"I could've helped." He hated the pleading note cutting through his voice. "You meant everything to me." Mac's breath whooshed out. Blood roared in his ears. It wasn't true. It couldn't be true. He'd never seen Tenley touch a drop of alcohol.

"I know." She lifted her head, showing the slim line of her throat. "And I would have destroyed us. Best-case scenario, you'd have pulled me over and been forced to give me a DUI. Worst case, we'd have kept going until I eventually ended up being the one causing a wreck like Dad's, like the one that put him in that wheelchair, or worse, Mac."

"But you didn't."

Tenley spun around. "No. And I thank God every day that He helped pull me out before then." She took a slow breath. "This isn't about me. This is about you understanding what I did." He shook his head, but she kept going. "I know you. Maybe better than you know yourself. You think it's your fault. No doubt you found a way to blame yourself and ran off to Chicago. You go somewhere and hide until the pain is manageable. I look at myself in the mirror every day and know that I'm the reason you left. Don't put this on me. I don't have the strength to carry it all."

"I'm trying to understand. But you're part of this too."

"No. You're trying to protect yourself. Life happens, Mac. Grief and love and death and joy. They're all part of it. You don't get one without the other. Do you know how many times I've looked at Dad and wished it was me in the car that night? I'm the one who should be paralyzed. I'm the one who made all the mistakes." She rubbed the cuff of her sleeve over her eyes, the movement angry as she dashed tears away, her hands shaking.

"That isn't your fault." He had to get her to understand that.

Zeus whined from his spot under the table but didn't emerge. The sound reminded Mac that Jade slept just down the hall. Jade. His blood turned cold. "You didn't tell me this before. Why?"

"Because you were looking for any reason to take Jade away from me. Telling you this is the proverbial smoking gun." She looked as tortured as he felt. "I loved you enough to drive you away. You got along fine without me." A rueful smile tipped her lips.

"That's what you think?" He let his arms fall to his sides. "Nothing has ever hurt me more than losing you." Not even Laura's death. He felt abominable over that, but it was the truth. He'd loved Laura with his whole heart, but Tenley was first, Tenley was now, always Tenley. She was his one and only. "Maybe things would have turned out the way you say." He brushed a hand down his face, dragging in a ragged breath. "But you didn't trust me enough to let me try."

"Alcoholism isn't a problem you could fix for me." Tenley pursued the same line of thought with dogged determination. "It was my battle. My choice. I had to want it, Mac. And with you there offering help at every turn, I knew I'd never quit. There was no reason for me to give it up as long as you were there."

"You didn't let me protect you." The crux of the problem rushed out of him. His shoulder throbbed as though he'd been shot all over again. His throat constricted. "That's all I ever wanted. To love you and protect you for the rest of my life."

"Sometimes, we have to protect ourselves." Tenley took a step toward him. Her hand lifted like she might touch his face. A tortured look entered her eyes, and she moved away. "I understand if you still want to take Jade to Chicago." Her voice dropped to a whisper. "I won't fight you on it. You're right. I don't deserve the chance to take care of her."

"You're giving up?" He scoffed. The bitterness in the sound echoed around the kitchen. "You fought me tooth and nail. You insisted that we could work this out. Now you're quitting?"

She lifted one shoulder to her ear and let it drop. "I love her enough to make sure she has the best life possible. Who wants an alcoholic as a stand-in mother? Amber wouldn't want that."

"Don't." He held up a hand. "Don't you dare say what my sister would want." Indecision warred inside him. "Did Amber know?"

Tenley flinched, and Mac had his answer.

"I'm a fool. Everyone knows. Everyone but me." His head fell forward, chin thumping against his chest. "The one person who you should've been able to trust is the one you pushed away." He spun on his heel. "Well, you don't have to worry about it anymore. I understand now." She'd never trusted him with her whole heart, with all her fears and her troubles. She'd withheld those pieces of herself and only given him the side she thought he could handle.

It was too much betrayal. He didn't know where they were supposed to go from here. When he first came back to Tamarack Springs, it was with the sole purpose of getting Jade back to Chicago. The longer he stayed, the more he remembered why he loved this place and the people who lived here.

For a few brief flashes, he'd remembered why he loved Tenley, and the desire to push her away had waned. It returned now in full force. He'd never asked anything of her, except that she love him. And she couldn't do that. She pushed him away and chose to suffer through her troubles alone.

Longing filled him. More than a desire to care for Jade and protect Tenley. More than a need to save. This need split his heart wide open. A need to be loved.

"Take care, Mac." Tenley's voice sent a shot of adrenaline through his veins.

He spun to face her, taking in her neutral expression and hands shoved deep into her purple hoodie. His gaze traveled down to her feet. Purple socks. He'd missed it before but saw it all clearly now.

Sadness sat in the room with them, filling the air with a gummy feeling that clung to him like cobwebs.

Mac nodded, forcing himself back to the conversation. What now? The ache intensified. It used to be easy, knowing what to say to Tenley.

The chasm between them yawned deep and wide. One step and he'd fall in, never to be seen again. Loving Tenley was fraught with peril. This time, he'd be going in with a full arsenal of equipment to keep him safe.

Love was never safe.

Exciting. Terrifying. Never safe. Not for him.

"I'm sorry for being blunt." Tenley had retreated behind a mask of indifference.

He stood frozen in the center of her kitchen. "You said what you needed to say."

Tenley ran her hand down his arm and grasped his fingers. "But I have something to say now that I couldn't say then. I love you, Mac. Always."

His breath rushed out, leaving him empty for a flash of time before a shining light took up residence in his chest and bloomed outward. "We can't, Ten. Too many obstacles, remember?" But, oh, how he wanted to believe it could happen.

"The only thing standing between us is the past. A list of wrongs I committed and the pain I caused." She pressed something hard into his palm. "I'm not going to chase after you and beg. But I'll be here. If you can forgive me, you know where to find me."

He stepped away, choked back a sob he was sure Tenley's parents could hear from their house. Tenley's face— her beautiful face—crumpled.

He cleared his throat, rubbed angry fists across his eyes, stalked across the living room, slapping his leg for Zeus to follow. "I have an appointment with Leonard on Monday. We'll sort this out then, but I'm taking Jade with me." If he stayed here one more minute, he didn't know what he'd do.

Keep telling her she'd made a mistake.

Say something he couldn't take back.

Kiss her until the world stopped spinning.

Everything he'd thought he knew about them, about their love, was false. How did he come to terms with that?

Tenley followed him into Jade's room and stood in the hallway while he scooped the little girl up and held her close. She muttered in her sleep but quieted when he told her where they were going.

Throughout the walk from the house to the truck, he waited for Tenley to argue. She remained silent as stone. Giving up. It made no sense to him that she'd fight so hard only to quit now. Maybe because she knew she'd never win if he contested the will. *When.* When he contested the will.

He'd wanted to trust Tenley with Jade's well-being, but she'd broken his trust too many times.

Once Jade was buckled in his truck, he pried his fingers open. Resting against his palm, he found the wedding band she'd bought for him. The black titanium band glinted in the moonlight, the softness of the color contrasting the strength of the material. Like Tenley. Like himself and the riotous feelings for Tenley that always resided in his heart.

Chapter Twelve

Confession was supposed to be good for the soul. So why did she feel so bad? Tenley rubbed her fists into her eyes, grinding out the scratchy feeling left over from the hours of crying. Her phone trilled her alarm for church, eliciting a groan. She rolled over and covered her head with her pillow. She didn't want to leave the house, much less explain to her family why her eyes were red.

That was the easy part.

She had to tell them about Jade. She and Mac were probably well on their way to Chicago by now. He'd said he wanted to talk to Leonard on Monday, but she knew that once he took a second to think, he'd decide to leave Tamarack Springs.

They were both too good at running away.

Tenley's phone shrilled again, this time with a text message. She groaned and rolled over, grabbing the phone and scanning the message before thumbing off a response to Mom that she'd not forgotten about dinner after church. She considered feigning an excuse not to go but rolled to her feet and resigned herself to the inevitable.

She managed to get through church without any problems other than a few concerned glances. Brody caught her elbow on the way out the door. Tenley tugged her arm free once they reached the parking lot. "Sheesh. Does Callie let you manhandle her like that?" She frowned at her brother.

"What's going on?" He leaned in close, his concerned gaze almost undoing her control.

She puffed her cheeks full of air and let it out in a slow exhale. "I can't talk about it here." She angled her head toward the crowd of curious onlookers.

Brody glanced back and nodded once. "We'll see you at dinner."

Not a question but a demand. She was surrounded by stubborn men who wanted to protect her. Good grief. Was she really going to complain about that?

Yeah. Kind of.

An urge to grin caught her by surprise. Tenley coughed to cover it and slipped into her truck to follow the rest of her family back home.

By the time they'd all gathered in the kitchen around plates of pot roast and root vegetables with fresh sourdough bread on the side, Tenley's stomach was a writhing mass of tangled knots.

Brody caught her eye. Under the table, his boot thudded against her calf.

Tenley scowled at him. "Mom, Brody's kicking me."

"Brody." Mom admonished with a wry twist to her lips.

"Tenley has something to tell us." He cocked his head to the side. "Don't you."

Again, not a question but a demand.

Tenley tightened her grip on the hem of her shirt.

Callie looked back and forth, her eyes wide. "Oh, this can't be good. Last time Tenley made that face was the day Brody put a frog under her hat."

Molly snickered into her napkin. Luke's gaze bounced from adult to adult. "Where's Jade?"

Tenley's heart lurched in her chest. She gave Brody a pleading look as tears welled in her eyes. She choked them back, but not before Brody fully understood what was about to happen.

"Jade's with Mac." Brody smiled at Luke, then shot a look at Molly that she understood right away.

Molly scooted her chair closer to Tenley and took her hand.

"I told Mac everything." Tenley forced her throat to keep working. "I'm not sure what happens next. He said he'd talk to Leonard tomorrow." But he'd not shown up at church, which was a big red flag. He'd promised to bring Jade to church.

She couldn't look at her family and see the disappointment. She scooted away from the table, her chair scraping the linoleum in a harsh screech. Her legs wobbled as she stood and made her way to Dad. She fell to her knees by his side and put her forehead on his arm. "I'm sorry. It's my fault. If I'd never called you that day, none of this would've happened. It's my fault you were hit." She might be a different person if not for that one choice.

"Don't." Dad put a hand on the back of her head and stroked her hair. "Don't you dare blame yourself for any of this. You made your mistakes, and you paid the price for them."

"That doesn't mean I shouldn't suffer the fallout. You're in that chair because of me. Amber went out that night because of me. Mac's leaving, or is already gone, because of me." And he took Jade with him. She didn't say that part, not with Luke listening in, but they all understood the implications.

"Mac's angry." Brody spoke up. His voice carried a weight to it, an understanding. "Once he has time to think things through, he'll come around." The assurance might've worked if Brody didn't reach for Callie's hand and squeeze like his life depended on it.

"If you're asking me for forgiveness, then you have it. You've had it all along because I never blamed you." Dad put a finger under Tenley's chin and lifted her head. "I love you. No matter what. Everyone is responsible for their own decisions. You couldn't know what would happen, and I would do it all again if it meant keeping you safe."

"But I was safe. I called you, then I changed my mind and went to the party anyway." Tenley sniffed back tears. "If I'd just stayed. If I'd waited for you to get there."

"Then we both might've been in the car when the driver crossed the yellow line." Dad kissed the top of her head. "The world is full of what-ifs and maybes. You can't play that game, Tenley. It's one that everyone loses. Make peace with yourself, forgive yourself, and keep moving toward God."

Keep moving toward God. The words hit a sweet note in her heart and resonated.

Small arms wrapped around Tenley's neck. Luke hugged her tight. "Love you bunches, Aunt Tenley."

"I love you too, squirt." She patted his arms and did her best to let go of the past that had hounded her every step for the last ten years. She'd tried to make up for it. The equine center became part of that, but it also felt like the thing she'd always been meant to do. She pushed to standing, grabbed Luke's feet, and carried him up with her.

Luke laughed and squeezed tighter.

Tenley bounced him a few times before detaching his arms and returning him to his chair. She eyed her family. "I'm going down to the barn." Her throat worked in a hard swallow. Tears blurred her vision, and she bolted.

Her breaths turned ragged by the second step down the long driveway. A sob worked its way up her throat and slipped out against her will. Dad forgave her. He'd never even blamed her. The weight she'd carried for ten years lifted. Tenley released it with a gulp of honeysuckle-scented air and stumbled into the barn.

Horses shuffled, a few of them poking their noses over the doors to watch her. Tenley scratched foreheads and patted sleek necks on her way down the aisle. She slipped into Shadow's stall, breathed deep through her nose and buried her face in Shadow's neck. The mare chuffed and ground hay but submitted to her affections.

"Tenley?" Brody stopped at the stall door, his eyes hidden beneath heavy brows.

"I'm sorry." She combed Shadow's mane with her fingers. "I understand if you can't forgive me."

Brody's long exhale lasted a full ten seconds. "I'm sorry too. I was so angry with Callie that I missed it. I didn't see that you needed help. I didn't want to look too hard at what you were doing. Growing up, you were always the pesky sister tagging along, begging to do everything I did."

Yep. She'd been like that. Her lips quirked at the memory. "And Molly spent all her time in the kitchen, learning how to bake."

"Well, you quoted lines from books all the time. I guess we all have our own quirks." Brody shifted his weight and cleared his throat. "When I figured out you were drinking, I told myself that it was nothing serious. That you'd outgrow it once you realized it was wrong. I had no idea you'd been drinking for years."

The knot in her throat swelled. "Then Dad got hurt and Callie left." She stepped away from Shadow and angled toward her brother. "I wish I'd made different choices." A shudder twitched her shoulders. Shadow nuzzled the middle of Tenley's back as though to offer comfort. "I should have been here to help you that night. I should have done a lot of things different."

"I knew you'd been invited to a party." Brody removed his hat and whacked it against his leg. "I'm as much to blame as you. I should've stepped in and made you come home. I thought maybe you'd choose your family." The words were caustic, but his soft tone said he meant them with earnest hope. "I wanted my sister back. The one who rode horses with me and nagged me every day because she was fearless in ways I wasn't."

"I'm beginning to think fearlessness is not a desirable trait for me."

"It is when it means you're not afraid to go after what you want." Brody looked at her, long and hard. "You still love Mac."

"It's too late for me and Mac." Her heart raced, the pitter-patter of adrenaline kicking in among the unfurling anger. "He doesn't trust me."

"Neither did I. Not for a long time after you came back from rehab. But you never stopped trying to prove you were worth trusting. Don't stop with Mac either." He offered a sad smile. "And I'm not mad at you. I've never apologized for all the things I've said over the years, or the way I treated you. I was mad at myself for not seeing it sooner."

"Seeing what?" She leaned against Shadow's shoulder and let every breath bring a release to the pain.

Brody settled his forearms on the stall door. "That you had a problem. I was so focused on my life, on keeping the ranch going, that I neglected you. I let you fend for yourself instead of offering a lifeline."

"It wasn't your place to save me." Just like it wasn't Mac's. Something the men in her life never seemed to understand. "I had to reach my own breaking point. I had to want sobriety for myself and no one else." She focused on talking through the pain cinched around her heart. "The responsibility was never yours to carry, big brother."

"Maybe Dad's right on this one."

Big words for Brody. He'd been the epicenter of anger around which Tenley revolved. Realization settled in. She'd wanted his approval the way she wanted Mac's trust. With acceptance came loyalty. With loyalty came love. With love came an end to the torment.

"How do we forgive?" The question tumbled out. "The person who hit Dad and then ran? I've tried to forgive them, but it's even harder than forgiving myself."

Brody stared down the barn aisle, a crease between his eyes. "I don't know. But I think we should try."

"It's a decision you'll have to make a thousand times over." Molly bounded into the barn, her sunshine heart spreading waves of love through the chill in Tenley. Molly had suffered the same as the rest of them, with the added pain of losing her husband the year Luke was born, yet she never lacked a restorative spirit.

"And you've done it. Just like that?" Curiosity drew Tenley closer to her younger sister. "You've forgiven them." *And me?* Tenley left off the last bit. Now wasn't the time to bring the conversation back to her and her troubles. This was the first time they'd discussed forgiveness for Dad's accident. Ever. She wasn't about to ruin it with her own insecurities.

"I'm trying." Molly scrunched her nose and shrugged. "I was angry, but then I realized that my anger doesn't affect them. It only makes me more miserable. I can't afford more misery. Luke has enough instability in his life. I won't add more."

Short and sweet, Molly's argument silenced the older siblings. Tenley glanced at Brody, who stared at Molly as though she were a different species. "I have the weirdest family."

Tenley tossed Molly's words around, examining them from every angle. She'd heard similar before, about forgiveness not being for the person who'd done wrong but for the one wronged. The Bible said that a person should forgive not seven times but seventy times seven. That didn't sound right. How did a person just keep forgiving? Tenley frowned and twisted her cuff. If she forgave, who received the bigger gift?

Pressure built behind her eyes, and she scrubbed the gritty feeling away with her palms. Bitterness and anger led to hatred. Hatred helped no one.

Now she was getting somewhere.

What difference might she feel if she let go? Tenley offered a tentative prayer for relief, while making a conscious decision to make the next few minutes free of thoughts of revenge.

An image of her mornings at the library flitted through, of the kids who tromped in and out every Saturday. They were young, with all of life ahead of them. Mistakes were part of life. Some of them would choose to take the wrong path. They'd need forgiveness. Everyone needed forgiveness. God gave it freely.

"What do you want out of life?" Molly joined Brody at the door. "Do you want to keep going with this hovering over your head, or do you want to give it up and let go?"

What did she want? What woke her up each morning and was her last thought before bed at night?

Peace. The word drifted on a cloud, too high to reach. But she wanted it. Oh, how she wanted peace.

Shadow nudged Tenley's back. Her shuffle brought her head around to Tenley's chest, where she butted her nose into Tenley's stomach.

Brody hitched up his jeans. "I'm going for a ride." His swagger carried him away at a rapid clip. "Got some thinking to do."

"Yeah." Tenley stroked Shadow's neck. "Me too."

Molly held out a hand to Tenley. Tenley gripped her sister's fingers. "Thank you." Her voice broke.

Molly nodded and smiled through a glint of tears in her eyes. "Mac will come around." She cleared her throat. "Don't give up. You tried that once. Maybe this time you fight for Mac like you fought for your sobriety."

Did she dare?

Mac sat on the back porch with his legs stretched down the steps and his heels resting on the ground. Jade ran across the backyard, Zeus at her side. She'd asked about Rascal, but Mac hadn't been able to bring himself to drive back to Tenley's to collect the pup.

His thoughts ran ahead of him, and no matter how many times he brought them back, he couldn't corral them into anything that made sense.

He felt betrayed by his sister and the entire Jacobs family. Tenley especially. That hurt worst of all.

"Got a minute?" The deep baritone came from the gate to Mac's right. He wheeled and found Brody sitting astride a horse, his wrists crossed over the saddle horn.

Mac considered denying Brody entry, but he knew it wouldn't do any good. Like Tenley, Brody had a tenacity that meant he'd sit there all night if he had to. Better to let him say whatever he'd come here to say and get it over with. He stood and opened the gate.

Brody dismounted and looped the horse's reins around one of the posts that anchored the picket fence. He followed Mac to the porch and waved at Jade, who ran over and hugged Brody's legs before loping off again.

Zeus gave Brody a cursory look and sniff before following Jade.

Mac sat and let the silence stretch. Best interrogation technique he'd ever learned. The guilty despised silence. Not that he wanted to interrogate Brody. Much. Questions about Tenley pinged around. He'd skipped church this morning to keep from coming in contact with her or her family. That hadn't stopped him from pouring out questions to God in prayer. Questions that were still unanswered.

"You leaving again?" When Brody finally spoke, concern carved a groove between his eyes. He removed his hat and settled it on his knee as he lowered to the step.

Mac stared across the yard. "I don't know."

"Fair enough." Brody settled in, and the sudden quiet surrounding them reminded Mac of why he and Brody had become natural friends. They knew when to leave the other to their thoughts and when to push. Brody plucked a blade of grass from the yard and twirled it between his thumb and forefinger. "Sorry I never told you."

"Family comes first." Mac let the weight of the words carry across the distance. "You were trying to protect her. I might not agree with what you all did, but I understand it." He shook his head. "That's not true. I'm furious. With Tenley. With all of you. You were my best friend aside from Tenley. Why wouldn't you tell me what she was going through?"

Brody frowned and leaned back, anchoring his elbows on the porch and stretching out his legs. "When Tenley came home the day of your wedding, she was a mess. Not just from the alcohol, but from realizing what she'd done. I've never seen her like that before. Not just the crying but the pure devastation. She was adamant that no one talk to you."

"And you agreed?" Mac snorted, disbelief evident in his tone.

"No." Brody met Mac's gaze, his own hard as steel. "After you left the barn, I drove Tenley to rehab. Stayed with her as long as I could. I was going to tell you when I got back. By then, you were gone." There was an accusation there, but Mac brushed it away. Brody drummed his fingers on the porch, the rapid beat revealing the tension he'd kept under wraps until now.

"We all made mistakes that weekend." Mac managed to admit.

"Well, maybe Tenley's stronger for having made this one." Brody stilled. "Took her a long time to hit the bottom and decide she wanted to claw her way out."

"And she wanted to do it without me." Mac sent a pointed look at Brody. "But you all were allowed to stay. You all knew. My sister knew."

A bark of laughter shook Brody's shoulders. "I see why you're in a knot now. Yeah, Amber knew. Not at first. Tenley told her about the same time you proposed to Laura. By then, Amber decided it was best if you didn't know. Said you'd found happiness finally."

"Yep." Mac squinted into the fading light and watched Jade throw a ball for Zeus. The pair were inseparable now.

What kind of relationship would they have if Tenley

refused to let him help her? He wanted her to need him. As a partner throughout the rest of their lives.

Brody knocked his bootheels on the ground, the expression on his face growing serious. "Tenley has a hard time admitting when she needs help."

Did that mean she needed help now and wouldn't admit it? Much as he tried to stop it, Mac's chest tightened. Would he always feel this way? Worried that the next words out of someone's mouth would be to warn him that Tenley was drinking. He'd known for all of a day and the worry threatened to drown him. He held his breath and waited.

"What is with you two and not breathing? Tenley nearly turned purple this morning when she told us you'd taken Jade and left." Brody shook his head. "Don't make me jab you, because I will. Y'all are worse than toddlers, holding your breath like it'll change things. I just wanted to tell you that she still needs you. Don't know if you're interested in sticking around, but you're welcome to."

Mac released his breath with a deep sigh. "Your parents don't mind?" He chuckled. "Why'd that sound like I was asking if they'd let me take Tenley out on a date?"

"One has nothing to do with the other. But no, they don't. They're thrilled you're back. They just worry. Parental rights, I guess. Tenley is happier when you're around." He bumped his shoulder into Mac's. "And I've missed having my friend." He held his hand up, thumb and finger pressed together. "Just a little bit. We've had precious little happiness lately and there have been more smiles since you came home."

Mac stood.

Brody's next words stopped Mac cold. "Callie told me something last week, and it really stuck with me."

"Yeah? What's that?"

"It's the people we love the most who hurt us the most." Brody lurched to his feet, and he strode away, leaving Mac with his mouth hanging open.

He loved Tenley. Had never stopped loving her. But this love went deeper and had grown stronger since his return. What did Tenley need from him? Would it be better if he left it alone and let her move on? He thought maybe he understood Tenley better now. He understood why she might think letting him go was the best answer. But Mac could not restart this relationship with Tenley unless he felt absolutely certain he could be there for every hurdle.

Loving Tenley meant risking himself. His heart belonged to her, but did he have the strength to offer his trust after everything she did?

If she didn't answer his calls one night, would he immediately leap to conclusions and accuse her of drinking?

He was so afraid of losing her, of losing another person he loved, that he couldn't think past the panic. Brody's tack jangled as he mounted up and rode away.

"Uncle Mac, I can't find my stuffed horse." Jade's wheedling tone caused Zeus to whine.

Mac raised his head and found Jade standing in the middle of the yard. "Where did you have it last?"

Her face scrunched into a frown. "I was throwing it for Zeus since I lost his ball." She shrugged. "I didn't see where it went."

Mac stood and stretched. "I'll help you look."

"Can't Zeus find it?" Jade motioned at the dog lying in the grass nearby.

"Zeus isn't a tracker. He doesn't find things." Mac held out his hand to Jade "Come on. We'll look together."

"I wanted Zeus to get it." Jade pouted. "Zeus, find the

horse." She mimicked one of Mac's hand motions, the one that sent Zeus away. He'd used it that night when he'd thought someone broke into Tenley's house.

Jade must have been awake and seen him.

Zeus lifted his head and whined. He licked his lips and sat up, attention riveted on Mac.

"Look, he wants to help." Jade tried again. "Zeus, find."

"He doesn't understand." Mac squeezed her fingers. "Zeus's specialty is protection."

Zeus stood and nosed the ground. His tail swished high in the air and he spun in a circle then streaked toward the fence.

"He'll find it." Jade gave a decisive nod. "I believe in him."

Oh, the faith of a child. Mac pressed his lips tight to keep from saying anything that might hurt Jade's feelings.

He wouldn't hurt her for the world.

You know where to find me. Tenley's voice ricocheted through his head, giving him freedom to move. He knew what he needed to do, but it would take time. It felt wrong to leave without saying goodbye, too much like a repeat of the past or an attempt to teach Tenley a lesson. It was neither.

He needed to prove that he was in it for the long haul. Words were not sufficient for that.

Jade squealed. "He did it!" She jumped up and down, pulling on his arm.

Mac squinted at the dog racing toward him with a fuzzy stuffed animal in his mouth. The dog ran to Jade and sat.

"Drop it." Jade pointed at the ground.

Zeus opened his mouth and the stuffed horse hit the ground.

"Good boy." Jade threw her arms around Zeus's neck and loved on him. "See. He just needed me to believe in him."

The next morning, Mac settled Jade into the seat beside him. Leonard sat across from them, his gnarled hands knotted together atop the desk. His gray suit was rumpled, and his tie hung slightly crooked, but his demeanor was all business. "You're sure about this?" Leonard reached into a side drawer and removed a file. "Last time we spoke, you wanted a reason to change the current situation." He eyed Jade meaningfully. "Took me a while, but I found this."

Mac took the proffered folder and flipped it open. Images of Tenley's arrest record stared back at him in black-and-white. Lank hair hung around her face, and a dazed expression lingered in her haunted eyes. He didn't recognize this Tenley. She was a stranger to him. His stomach knotted. Until this moment, he'd been able to tell himself that it didn't matter. Maybe it was even a ruse from Tenley to push him away. He couldn't deny it any longer. He had undeniable proof. Mac scanned the document that listed Tenley's infraction as drunk-and-disorderly, snapped the folder shut and handed it back to Leonard. "We don't need that. I've made up my mind."

Leonard's weathered and worn face creased into a smile. He patted the desk with both hands. "Well then. Let's get on with it." He retrieved a stack of forms and grabbed a pen.

Jade fidgeted in her seat as boredom settled in. Mac watched her from the side while he answered Leonard's questions and then signed the paperwork.

Leonard held out a hand to Mac. "If it means anything, I think you made the right choice."

Mac let his own grin match Leonard's as he shook the older man's hand. "Coming from you, that means a lot."

Leonard held up a hand to halt them when Mac stood and reached for Jade's hand. "Before you go, I have something for Jade." He removed the lid on a crystal candy dish, revealing an assortment of mints.

Jade flashed a questioning look at Mac, then grabbed a green peppermint when he nodded. She popped the candy into her mouth and spoke around it. "Can we see Tenley now?"

Mac winced slightly. "Not yet. There are a few more things to take care of." He snuck a look at his phone and the unanswered calls from his captain in Chicago. They were increasing in frequency, and Mac knew he walked a thin line, ignoring the calls.

Once they were in his truck and headed toward the Jacobs' family ranch, Mac tried to relax. Everything was moving as it should. According to Brody, Tenley was at the Wells's ranch with Callie. Which meant Mac and Jade could visit Margaret and Peter before they left town.

Jade bounced in her seat. "Are we going to take Rascal with us?"

"Not this time." Mac drummed his fingers on the wheel. "Tenley will take care of him until we get back."

Jade puckered her lips in a grimace but didn't argue. She waited for him to stop the truck before she unsnapped her seatbelt and grabbed for the door handle.

Mac followed Jade up the steps and rapped his knuckles on the front door.

Margaret answered with a smile and pushed open the squeaky screen. "Come on in. You don't have to knock, Mac." She swatted at him with a kitchen towel. "You're family. Same as always." Mac followed Margaret into the kitchen, where Peter sat at the table working on a saddle. He glanced up when Mac entered and grunted a hello. "Almost done, Mac. Brody needed these fenders replaced weeks ago, but he's not had the time."

"No rush." Mac took a seat and waited.

Jade scampered over to Margaret, her chatter filling the kitchen.

Peter poked the leather strap of a new fender through the saddle tree and pulled. The leather slid home with a snap, and he picked up the stirrup from in front of Mac. "Brody gave us the rundown on what's happening." He lifted one bushy eyebrow. "Sounds like a good plan." A beat of silence, then, "Not sure of your motives."

"Sad fact is, I'm not sure of them either. But I know I have to go back to Chicago. Wrap up things that need tending." He tugged the old saddle fender out of Peter's way and ran his hand along the ragged edge of leather that would've snapped soon. Only a matter of time. That's what it all came down to. Time. "I need to clear my head. Make sure this is what I want, but this place—" he made a vague motion with his hand "—this town, it gets to you, you know? I'm too close."

"I get that." Peter buckled the hobble strap around the fender and scrubbed a knuckle over his cheek. "Can you look me in the eye and tell me you're not running off without telling Tenley as some way of punishing her? Of punishing us in asking that we keep this from her?"

Mac met the older man's gaze. "Peter, you've been like a father to me since high school. I'd never ask you to hurt Tenley. I'll be back." The truth of it landed between them. He was coming back. Back to Tenley. Back home where he belonged.

Peter's gaze followed Mac when he stood. Once full

and jovial, the older man's cheeks were now sunken, the cheekbones sharp.

His smile never changed, and it appeared now as a rainbow after a storm. "That's the Mac I remember. Sit and talk a while."

How did he keep positive? Mac sat, lowered his hands to his knees, and pressed his back into the chair. "Sorry I didn't come back sooner." The response came without thought, but Mac realized as it left his lips that he meant it.

"I'm not going anywhere." Peter chuckled at his own joke before growing serious. "Tell me, son. What do you want from Tenley?"

Restitution. Forgiveness. Tenley. Each word battered harder than the one previous. Had he come back for her? He'd not thought so. Not when he first arrived. He'd come back for Jade. But he knew, deep in his heart, he knew that a part of him had hoped for reconciliation.

The moment Tenley walked into his life, things shifted. She became the center of his life. Her gravity hauled him in and put him in orbit so that he saw her. Only her. He broke away from the black hole of Tenley's grasp.

"Jade." Mac spoke past the lump in his throat. "I came back for her. To make sure she had a good life." And that she'd not be in Tenley's life. "I'm sorry I left the way I did. When Tenley and I—"

Mr. Jacobs shook his head. "There's no need for you to apologize for that. You had to protect yourself. I know it. Tenley knows it. She doesn't care to think about it, but she knows it." He cleared his throat and blinked away tears. "She's a strong woman, Mac. Stronger than any of us truly know. When she's taken with something, nothing will stand in her way."

How well he knew. Even when she chose to focus on the wrong thing.

"Do you think she'll ever forgive me?"

"I think she already has. I saw how she looked at you. That girl loves you."

A memory of Tenley curled into all the empty places in his heart. He'd missed her. Every waking moment during their years apart. Her presence righted his trajectory. But could he trust her? Did he have the strength to love her again, knowing each day was a precipice, a knife edge, between her and sobriety?

The amount of trust required sapped his strength. *This is why cops don't marry criminals.* Unfair though it was. Divorce rates among cops were sky-high. Tenley might be a criminal in the milder sense of the word, but deep in the archives of Bridgeport's police department, a file with her name on it and a list of infractions remained.

He'd seen it for himself, and even now, doubt tried to wiggle its way in.

Mac slammed the door on his fears and stood. "Let's go, Jade. I'm going to need your help in Chicago."

Chapter Thirteen

Tenley wanted to hug the early morning sunshine. One week with forgiveness for herself clashed with missing Mac and Jade. The conflicting emotions overwhelmed her, growing stronger every day. She needed this run more than ever. She hurried through a series of stretches before setting out in a ground-eating trot. Knowing she'd regret the pace, she pushed her legs faster. Maybe, if she ran fast enough, she could outrun the past…and the pain.

She'd messaged Mac to no avail. Voicemails went unanswered. She'd driven over to Amber's house, but the windows were dark and the front door locked. Mac's truck gone from the driveway. He'd retreated to Chicago, leaving her with little more than a quick note that he'd be in touch.

Thundering heartbeats slammed against her ribs. Dappled rays of sunlight flecked the trail, creating highlights of light and shadow, a masterpiece of color bouncing off thick tree trunks and beaming through the green leaves. Lungs burning, she passed the one-mile marker standing upright in the shade, a picket of success. Pine filled her nose with every breath, soft evergreen needles cushioning each pounding stride.

Clicking the timer button on her watch, she kicked the pace up another notch.

An ache settled below her right lung. *Breathe, Tenley.* In. Out. Repeat.

Pain seared her chest, lancing through like a thunderbolt as memories assailed her vision. Dad crumpled in a heap amid the wreckage. No sign of the person who'd crashed into his car. The doctor's prognosis and the paralysis. Mac's leaving. Never seeing Jade again. She bit her tongue to keep from screaming and increased her pace.

Another marker flashed by.

She ignored her watch. What did it matter? Time held no quarter here. It did not ease the agony.

A flash of color by her side wrestled her attention from the past. Mac. He nodded, mouth in a flat line, eyes bright. Brown hair flopped with every footfall. Tanned arms pumped in rhythm with her own. Their feet landed in sync, legs eating up the miles.

"Hi," he said simply.

Athletic shorts and a blue tank top said he'd meant to be here today. Looking for her? He couldn't possibly know that she'd be here, running the trails at the ranch. Unless he'd planned it. Which meant that he'd talked to her family.

Confusion warred with a feeling of elation. What was he doing here?

She gauged his breathing. Steady. Exerted, but no worse than her own.

He inclined his head, giving her permission to set the pace. They were already blistering their way down the trail, but Tenley accepted the challenge and kicked into her last gear as easily as a racehorse nearing the finish line.

Mac's back. Her footfalls landed in a jarring tempo that matched the refrain. *Mac's back. Mac's back. Mac's back.* Her heart soared. He wouldn't come here like this if he meant to break her heart. She'd told him that he knew where to find her, and now he had.

Mac raced beside her, never faltering or falling back.

Even though she wanted to be alone, she couldn't deny the security of long-ago friendship, giving her a glimmer of hope. How long since she'd allowed hope to sneak into her life?

He swiveled his head in her direction, switching between watching her and the trail.

Tenley read the concern in his expression. She'd never been one for exercise, but with sobriety on the line, she needed an outlet. Running gave her that. An escape, and an endorphin rush.

A slow grin spread across Mac's face. He eased a step ahead, a challenge. His warm acceptance traveled the length of her bones, spreading a heated glow that had nothing to do with exercise. Tenley shut it down and cranked out another gear. They didn't need words. It was enough that he was here. At her side.

Two miles later, the dirt path changed to grass, and Tenley checked her pace, dropping her speed every few feet until they reached the trail's peak. Tenley slowed to a fast walk until she reached the rock ledge jutting out over the valley.

Coming to a stop, she nodded a thanks at Mac. Questions bombarded her. Why had he come back? Did he want to stay? She longed to ask. Not yet, though his running with her today put in solid groundwork that might be built on if she allowed it. Did she want to allow it? A month ago, an adamant no would have burst out. After a week without him, a definitive yes crept in.

Side by side, they strolled to the edge. Rock crumbled beneath Mac's feet and fell into the void. A deep valley

spread out below the ridge, a forest of trees proudly showing off bright green foliage. Wind howled over the break,
whipping Mac's shirt against his chest and causing Tenley
to slap a hand on her ball cap to keep it from flying away.

Tenley dropped to the ground and dangled her feet over
the edge. "I never get tired of this view."

"Or of giving me heart palpitations every time you do
that." Mac rubbed his chest.

Patting the rock beside her, Tenley grinned at him.
"Come on. You don't have to put your feet over, just sit
here with me. You won't fall."

"You underestimate how much I'm shaking in my
shoes right now. I'd vibrate right off the edge like a Slinky
on stairs." He held out a hand to prove he wasn't kidding.
His fingers spasmed and jerked.

Her laughter filled the air. "Sorry. It isn't funny."

Mac slipped off a backpack that she hadn't noticed and
unzipped it. He pulled out two water bottles. Condensa-
tion trickled across his knuckles. He handed her one and
cracked the seal on the other. After taking a long drink,
storm-filled eyes locked on her. "You plan on setting the
same pace going back?"

Laughter slipped out before she could stop it. "Maybe."

"We need to talk first."

Pure, unadulterated fear pressed a hard ridge against
her spine. He'd seen her past, lived part of it with her, but
the darkest parts, the bits that chased her, always looking
for a way back into her life, those she could not let him
see. Her past impeded their ability to coexist. "Okay."

She saw their chance at reconciliation slipping away.
She reached for it. "I'm sorry I never told you. If I'd shared
my struggles with you, maybe things would've turned
out different."

"You used to tell me everything." He crushed the bottle in his hands, the plastic emitting a protest. "At least, I thought you did."

Step eight of the twelve-step program darted through her thoughts. *Made a list of all persons we had harmed and became willing to make amends to them all.* She was willing. The list under her pillow attested the fact. Step nine, though. That one made her grind her teeth. *Made direct amends to such people wherever possible, except when to do so would injure them or others.*

She'd apologized to him. Her explanation weighed the air between them. Even after their talk last week, she didn't feel like she'd properly explained herself. Not that it really made a difference, but she had to try.

Standing, she put a hand on his forearm. "I thought I was doing the right thing. I see now that I was selfish. I wallowed in my pain and kept it from you. I put on a front to the one person I knew I could trust with my whole heart. I pushed you away." She shook her head and tucked the water into the crook of her elbow so she could take Mac's hand in both of hers. "I wanted to save you from me, from the person I'd become."

His callused fingers wrapped around her wrist and squeezed. "Loving you was the only thing I ever wanted. We both made mistakes. If you'd told me about your alcoholism, I would have tried to save you. Like you said. Maybe we needed to go through this valley of trials."

Movement in the trees throughout the valley snagged Tenley's attention. "Like the seasons change, so too do the seasons of the heart." She firmed her resolve and met Mac's eyes. "I want a second chance, Mac. Let me prove to you that I can be worthy of forgiving."

"You don't need to earn forgiveness." Mac ran his thumb across her knuckles.

What did he mean? Was he not even going to give her a chance? "People change. Molly says that things about people change, even if the whole person is the same. This is something about me that has changed."

Giving her a look that said he wasn't going to back down, Mac sat on the overhang, either to show he'd overcome his fear or to prove her point about change, and patted the leftover space. "Talk to me."

Tenley took a breath and joined him. "I'm still in love with you." There. She'd said it. The words were out there, wild and free. Mac could do what he wanted with them. Maybe this time he'd listen.

She shot to her feet. It hurt too much to stay still. She needed movement, the slap of feet on packed dirt. The rush of air over her face and the pounding tempo of an exerted heart. Not this bludgeoning pain ripping her apart from the inside out. Does one ever recover from betraying family? So far, the answer was no. Though she'd not been the one behind the wheel, she could have been. It should have been her who took the injuries. Molly touted forgiveness as the key to moving forward.

How could Tenley forgive a stranger for ruining Dad's life when she couldn't forgive herself for the pain she'd inflicted on Mac?

Mac took her elbow, grounding her with him, here at the ridge. Every heartbeat drummed in her ears, the whoosh drowning out his words.

He peered into her face, then pulled her into his arms. Home.

It felt right, being here again. And that's why she couldn't stay. Tenley pulled away and bolted down the trail. He'd come back, but she wasn't worthy of a second chance.

Seconds later, Mac set his stride to hers and they ran together. Each step took her deeper into the past, dredging up history she'd rather stayed buried.

When she reached the edge of the forest and their old meeting place came into view, Tenley skidded to a halt and leaned over, planting her hands on her knees. Her breaths wheezed in and out. She'd not meant to come here. It hurt to stand in the place where the past saturated the heady air and know they didn't have a future. Not one that included the other. Mac still hadn't acknowledged her proclamation. She waited with bated breath.

"Ready for breakfast?" Mac stretched, bending his leg back in an arc. Unlike her, his breathing could barely be called labored. He looked ready to go again.

Tenley did her own stretches, her legs feeling more like wet noodles with each minute that passed. "You'd eat after a run like that?" Her heart fell. Here she'd offered him her everything and he was thinking about food.

Mac shrugged. "You keep running away every time we try to talk."

"Hey. You bolted after the homecoming." Tenley felt the need to point that out even as Mac smiled at her.

"Okay. So we're both good at running away." He stretched his other leg. "What if we both agreed to stop pushing the other away?"

Mac chuckled at the indignant expression Tenley gave him. He stretched his left arm across his torso, twisting at the waist, then repeated the movement with the other arm. "Join me?" He motioned at the bench.

The backpack scratched his skin through the thin shirt.

A lump burned in his throat when Tenley shot him a dis-believing look. "Please. You took off before I was done talking."

She huffed but settled on the stone bench that he'd built during their senior year in high school.

Mac slid the backpack from his shoulders and dropped it onto the ground before moving to sit beside Tenley. He stretched out his legs, attempting to relax the jumping muscles.

Tenley rolled her head from side to side, then stretched her arms over her head. "What did you want to say?"

His grin returned. "You're just as impatient as I re-member."

She punched his shoulder. "I said I still loved you, and you didn't answer. Then you packed up Jade and left town. I said it again and you ignored me. Forgive me if I'm not in the mood to kid around." She looked out over the val-ley. A sigh parted her lips. "I haven't been here in years."

"I remember the last time we sat here." Mac reached into the bag with one hand while draping his other arm across the back of the bench. Nerves attacked, and his fingers clenched around the papers he withdrew from the bag.

Tenley pinched her eyes closed. "You proposed here. We planned our wedding here. Our future. But all that's over now." She shifted sideways and drew her leg under-neath her. "Please, Mac. Don't draw this out. If this is some kind of punishment, please know that there's noth-ing worse you can do to me. Get it over with. Tell me you want to move on."

"Is that what you want?" He stilled as a cold chill washed down his spine. Had he waited too long? It had taken longer than he thought to get everything together.

No. She said she still loved him. He trusted the raw emotion in her voice and the pure terror in her eyes when he didn't respond. If he could go back, he'd react differently, but she'd surprised him.

"I'm glad you left." Each word Tenley spoke drove the wreckage deeper into his chest.

He fought for air. Mac kept silent. Waiting, hoping for forgiveness. For abandoning her when she needed him most.

"You're the one person I didn't destroy." Tenley placed a shaking hand on his arm. "I couldn't see it then. How much my drinking hurt you. I refused to see how it impacted Brody and Molly. Mom and Dad. It wasn't until I came home from rehab that the veil lifted and I could see the trail of damage behind me. When I left, I was a mess. I had no idea what to do. I told myself for years that I made the right choice in driving you away."

Mac settled his hand on the back of her neck. "I want forever with you. That's all I've wanted since the day we started dating."

She blinked furiously. "I'm willing to fight for happily ever after. But only if you're willing to give me a chance. You said I can't earn your forgiveness. I understand that."

"You misunderstood me." Mac traced the curve of her jaw with his forefinger. "I said you didn't need to earn forgiveness. Because you already have it."

"Oh." She breathed the word into the narrow space between them.

Mac pulled the papers from behind his back and pressed them into her lap.

"What's this?" She eyed the tri-folded papers like she would a snake. Her expression flickered from worry, to panic, to hope and then to resignation. Moving cautiously, Tenley unfolded the notarized will and testament and began to read.

A hand came up to cover her mouth. "Is this real?" She ran a finger across the gold seal and the notary stamp. "Why would you make up a will?" Her eyes widened. "Mac?"

"If anything happens to me, I want you to have sole guardianship of Jade." He tapped the pages. "If you're willing to give me a chance to make up for leaving you when you needed me most."

Her chin trembled. "I'd give you a hundred chances."

"Good." Mac gave a decisive nod. "I'm moving back to Tamarack Springs. Sheriff Hanks offered me a spot with the department. Jade and I packed up my apartment in Chicago." He brushed a tendril of hair over her ear. "That's why I was gone. I needed to clear my head, away from the influence of this place and all the memories here. And I needed to get the papers drawn up."

A smile brightened her eyes, like sunshine was pouring out of her. She flung her arms around his neck and held on. "I love you."

"It's always been you, Tenley." He wrapped his arms around her waist and pulled her close. "I tried to scrub you out of my life, but you've always been there. You're rooted in my heart so deep that nothing could pull you out."

"Are you calling me a weed?" She laughed into the side of his neck.

He pulled back far enough to catch her gaze. "You're the most stubborn weed I've ever known. You're my first love, and God willing, my last." He hesitated. "If you'll have me."

"I wouldn't have it any other way."

His lips met hers, his eyes falling shut. The thrill of

love cascaded through him. This was what it meant to come home again. To find peace amid the storm and chaos that life had thrown his way. He'd thought his life and all the love in it gone forever. He'd lost everyone through the years and struggled to trust that love might be worth the threat of pain and loss.

With Tenley in his arms and their future stretching before them in a golden path studded with the memories of their past, he knew they'd make it. They were older, wiser and more willing to trust each other. The jagged pieces of their past hurts only made them stronger.

Epilogue

One year later.

Tenley rode alongside Mac up the winding trail carving its way through the forest of oak, maple and hickory trees. She tugged her hat brim down to shield her eyes as they emerged from the path and into the sunlight rising over the ridge. The sight took her breath away as pink and purple spread over the horizon. Her white dress fluttered in the breeze and the first rays of sunlight warmed her shoulders.

Zeus and Rascal trotted on either side of Jade as she rode ahead. Mac had done wonders for the pup in the last year, most of which he attributed to Zeus's calming influence. Mac's captain in Chicago had retired the K-9 and helped Mac through the process of adoption. Zeus spent his days playing with Jade and Rascal or loping alongside Tenley and Mac on their daily runs.

Mac reined his horse closer to Tenley and took her hand. They rode like that, boots and knees brushing with every stride, until they reached the outcropping. Jade waved and bounced in her saddle. "We're here!"

Laughter joined the sound of creaking leather as her family circled around. Jade rode over and stopped alongside Luke and Molly. Her dad turned his chair to face the approaching couple, her mother standing by his side.

Tenley felt a tug on her hand and glanced down, her gaze snagging on the engagement ring winking at her.

"Ready?" Mac grinned the mischievous smile from their youth, the one that sent her stomach tumbling and her heart racing. "I think it's time."

"Yeah?" She lifted an eyebrow. "What makes you say that?"

Mac motioned at her family—soon to be his too—and cupped a hand around his mouth. "Because I don't want to spend another day without you." He leaned in close enough to whisper. "I'm ready to see you walk down the aisle dressed in white, Tenley." He winked. "Or ride beside me all the way to the altar."

"Not afraid I'll bolt again?" After the last year of healing and growth, the previous insecurities didn't bait Mac into frowning.

He nudged his horse closer. "If you do, then this time, I'll follow you. And I won't stop until you do. We're in this together."

"I'm done running away from you, Mac." Her breath hitched. She nodded at the pastor waiting on horseback amid her family and their friends. "Today would've been our eight-year anniversary."

He squeezed her hand. "Everything worked out the way it was meant to."

"Just needed a little faith, trust and pixie dust." She winked at him and cupped his cheek. "You're all mine, cowboy."

"Always was." He answered before his lips touched hers.

"You're supposed to wait till he says the words," Luke piped in. He bounced in his saddle. "They're doing it wrong, Uncle Brody."

Brody grinned at Callie and tipped his hat in Tenley's direction. "I think we'll let it slide this one time."

The pastor grinned and cleared his throat. "Looks like we'd better get started."

Tenley looped her arm through Mac's and they nudged their horses forward amid whistles and cheers from all around.

Forever might not last as long as she wanted, but right now, with Mac by her side, it was long enough.

* * * * *

If you liked this story from Tabitha Bouldin,
check out her previous Love Inspired book:

The Cowgirl's Last Rodeo

Available now from Love Inspired!
Find more great reads at www.LoveInspired.com.

Dear Reader,

Thank you for taking a chance on Tenley and Mac's story. It's not every day that I get to work on a book that speaks so near and dear to my heart.

This one was a struggle from start to finish, but Tenley and Mac pushed me to keep going until I got it right. This story of second chances, redemption, and healing old wounds brought up a lot of emotion during every rewrite and I love how it finally turned out.

Writing siblings is one of my favorite things. The way they all interact with each other is usually how I inject humor but also discuss serious topics. I hope you enjoy this journey with the Jacobs siblings.

Tabitha